Hesiod

Theogony
and
Works and Days

Theogony
and
Works and Days

Stephanie Nelson
Boston University

Richard Caldwell

Hesiod: Theogony and Works and Days
© 2009 Stephanie Nelson, Richard Caldwell

Focus Publishing/R. Pullins Company
PO Box 369
Newburyport MA 01950
www.pullins.com

Cover Design by Guy Wetherbee | Elk Amino Design, New England | elkaminodesign.com

ISBN 13: 978-1-58510-288-4

Printed in the United States of America

14 13 12 11 10 9 8 7 6 5

0712TS

Table of Contents

General Introduction

Richard Caldwell

Greece Before Hesiod

Hesiod and Homer did not invent writing, nor did they invent literature, but their works are the earliest surviving examples of Greek literature written down in the alphabetic script which the Greeks borrowed from Phoenicia, probably during the 8th century or shortly before. Once before the Greeks had possessed a method of writing, the syllabic script known as Linear B which the Myceneans adopted from Minoan Crete. The use of Linear B, however, seems to have ended with the destruction of Mycenean civilization 500 years before Hesiod, and in any case the surviving Linear B material contains nothing literary or mythological except for the names of a few gods, some of them familiar.

It is not only written literature which first appeared at the time of Hesiod; Greek history itself can be said to have begun during the 8th century. Everything before this time, despite the brief presence of Mycenean writing, is prehistoric in the sense that virtually all we know about the way people lived, including their religious beliefs and myths, is based on the physical remains studied by archaeologists and not on written records. For this reason almost everything said in the following survey of Greek prehistory is probable at best; the present state of our knowledge does not allow certainty in most matters, and in some of the most important does not even guarantee probability. This is not true, at least to the same extent, of the ancient Near East, where written records and literature existed long before the arrival of the first Greek-speaking people in Greece at the end of the third millennium. Nevertheless the question of influence and exchange between Greece and the East during the prehistoric period is still largely a mystery.

The Greek language is Indo-European; that is, it belongs to the large family of languages derived from a single language spoken by a hypothetical people who lived in northeast Europe or northwest Asia during the Neolithic period. In irregular waves of migration from the beginning of the third millennium to the middle of the second, descendants of this people spread throughout Europe and into central Asia as far east as India. One branch of these Indo-European

1

nomads, who spoke an early form of the language we now know as Greek, entered the mainland of Greece around the beginning of the second millennium. They presumably brought with them both poetry and a polytheistic religion in which the chief god was associated with fatherhood and the sky, since these are elements of the general Indo-European tradition. In Greece they met, probably conquered, and merged with a native people, the early Helladic culture of the beginning of the Greek Bronze Age; before the coming of the Greeks, metallurgy had been introduced into Helladic Greece from the east, just as agriculture, the domestication of animals, and the painting of pottery had come earlier to Greece from Mesopotamia through Asia Minor. We know hardly anything about Helladic religion, of which only a few figurines have survived; whether it may have resembled the religion of nearby Minoan Crete remains a guess.

When the first Greeks entered Greece, one of the great civilizations of the ancient world was already flourishing on the island of Crete to the south. This culture, known as Minoan after Minos, the mythical king of Crete, had been in contact with the Near East and Egypt during the 3rd millennium; thanks to these contacts (which were to increase greatly during the 2nd millennium), a favorable climate, and a protected location, the Minoans had developed a prosperous civilization with large unfortified cities, great royal palaces, and spectacular refinements in art and architecture. The Minoans also possessed writing in the form of a pictographic or hieroglyphic script which developed later into Linear A, the syllabary which the Mycenean Greeks adopted to write Greek. Since neither Minoan script has been deciphered, all our evidence for Minoan religion is pictorial and conjectural. A goddess (or probably goddesses, who may yet represent different aspects of one goddess), presumably associated with the earth and fertility, seems to be the dominant figure; male figures who may be gods appear, and later myths such as Hesiod's story of the infancy of Zeus on Crete (Th 468-484) may point to a Minoan myth of a son or consort (or both) of a goddess.

Within a few centuries of their arrival, the Greek rulers of the mainland came squarely under the influence of the Minoans. The power and cultural sophistication of the mainland increased rapidly through the Middle Helladic period and reached its height during the late Helladic period, the 16th through the 13th centuries. Meanwhile the Minoan civilization, at its greatest during the 17th and 16th centuries, went into decline after the destruction of the palaces, caused perhaps by the eruption of the volcanic island Thera around 1450.

The Late Helladic period, the final phase of the Bronze Age on the Greek mainland, is most commonly named the Mycenean period, since the city of Mycenae in the Peloponnesus seems to have been the most important Mycenean center (an assumption strengthened by the pre-eminence of Mycenae and its king Agamemnon in the myths of the Trojan War). The chief Mycenean cities — Mycenae, Tiryns, and Argos in the Argolis, Pylos in Messenia, Thebes and Orchomenus in Boeotia, Iolcus (modern Volos) in Thessaly, Eleusis and Athens in Attica, as well as Cnossus on Crete, which was taken over by the Myceneans during this period — all play a significant role in later myth, and it is this period which provides the setting for much of Greek myth as it was later known to Hesiod and Homer.

Minoan influence on Mycenean civilization is so extensive that the few exceptions stand out clearly. There is nothing in Crete like the battle scenes in Mycenean art, or the enormous Cyclopean fortifications which protect the Mycenean citadels (the archaeological term is derived from myths crediting the one-eyed giants called Cyclopes with building these walls; post-Mycenean Greeks did not believe that ordinary mortals could have lifted the great stone blocks). Mycenean frescoes, jewelry, pottery painting and shapes, and architecture (with such exceptions as the distinctive Helladic room-style called the megaron) imitated Minoan models so closely that it is often difficult to tell them apart. Whether the same assimilation applied to religion and myth is impossible to say; the iconographic evidence shows great similarity, but the absence of literary records makes these pictorial data difficult to interpret. The figure of a bull, for example, appears everywhere in the Minoan remains — on buildings, frescoes, pottery, and jewelry and in sacrificial, ritual, and athletic contexts — and the bull is very prominent in later Greek myths concerning Crete, but the exact connection between artifacts and myth is impossible to establish. In the case of Mycenean culture we have the advantage of written records in a known language, but since the Linear B tablets are almost entirely inventories and accounting records of the religious and political bureaucracy, all they can tell us are the names of some deities and the facts that sacrificial cults existed and that the religious system was highly organized.

Names on the Linear B tablets which correspond with gods and goddesses in later Greek religion include Zeus, Hera, Poseidon, Hermes, Enyalios (a double of Ares), Paiaon (an epithet of Apollo), Erinys (an epithet of Demeter, as well as the singular form of the three Erinyes or Furies), Eleuthia, and perhaps Athena, Artemis, Ares, Dione, and Dionysus. In addition, there is a goddess, or many goddesses, called Potnia ("lady" or "mistress"), a name occurring usually but not always with some qualification: Potnia of horses, Potnia of grain, Potnia of the labyrinth, etc. Finally there are several deities whose names do not appear later, such as Manasa, Drimios the son of Zeus, and Posidaija (a feminine form of Poseidon). The tablets, on a few of which these names appear, were found in great number at Cnossus and Pylos and in smaller quantities at Mycenae and

Thebes; they were preserved by the fires which accompanied the destruction of these sites during the 14th through 12th centuries.

The end of Mycenean civilization coincided with general disruption in the eastern Mediterranean area and may be due, at least partially, to the raids of the mysterious "Sea Peoples," who appear most prominently in Egyptian records. A major role may also have been played by the movement into central Greece and the Peloponnesus of new groups of Greek-speaking peoples from the northwest. Only Athens and its surrounding area, and a few isolated places in the Peloponnesus, escaped destruction.

Most survivors of this turbulent period probably remained in Greece but the level of culture changed radically; writing, building in stone, and representational art disappeared, and cultural depression and poverty were widespread, especially in the century or two immediately following the Mycenean collapse. A Mycenean group fled to the island of Cyprus; they were followed, toward the end of the 2nd millennium, by large-scale migrations from the Greek mainland to the eastern Aegean islands and the coast of Asia Minor. Aeolians from Boeotia and Thessaly moved into the northern part of this area, Ionians (a mixed group chiefly from Attica and Euboea, but perhaps including temporary refugees in Athens from other parts of Greece) occupied the central section, and Dorians settled in the south, including Crete. A cultural revival began in Athens around 1050, marked by a distinctive pottery style called Proto-Geometric, and gradually spread throughout the Greek world. Other than changes in the Geometric pottery series and a great increase in the use of iron during the 11th century, however, there is little we can say about Greek higher culture during the period 1200-800, appropriately called the "Dark Age" of Greece.

Nevertheless there seems to have been an extended period of relative calm and stability during the second half of the Dark Age, which resulted in a substantial increase in both population and prosperity by the end of this period and the beginning of the Archaic period (8th-6th centuries). By the time of Hesiod, during the first century of the Archaic period, Greece had entered into a cultural and economic revival of large proportions. Over-population was an important factor not only in political and economic change but also as an impetus for a great colonizing movement which spread Greek culture throughout and beyond the central and eastern Mediterranean during the Archaic period. More significantly, colonization introduced Greece to other cultures, and this acquaintance was accelerated by the rapid expansion of Greek trading relations, particularly with the Near Eastern civilizations of Syria and Phoenicia. An increasingly powerful merchant class arose, generating further political and economic change, and a wealth of new ideas poured into Greece from overseas, including coinage, the Orientalizing pottery style, the alphabet, and knowledge of eastern customs and myths. We cannot know to what extent Hesiod participated in these Archaic developments; the legends which appeared later about his travels cannot be verified, and the only real evidence we have is what is contained in the surviving poems. The only place we know he visited is Chalcis on Euboea, the long island which runs along the eastern borders of Attica, Boeotia, and Thessaly, scarcely ever more than a stone's throw from the mainland. Euboea was almost certainly an important center of cultural and poetic activity at Hesiod's time and before, and, because of its close contacts with the Near East, it was a place where eastern ideas could affect Aeolic and Ionic poetic traditions.

The headings of the sections in the following translation have been placed in brackets to remind the reader that these are the editor's invention and not Hesiod's. Lines bracketed within the text have been condemned by some editors as later additions. Names have been most often given in translation, occasionally with the Greek name supplied at the first occurrence, in parenthesis, as "Heaven (Ouranos)". In the case of minor deities the meaning of the name has often been added, as " Euterpe, the Well Delighting". Although it has not been possible to keep one English word for one Greek word in the translation, the index indicates where a particular word has been used, such as *plutus* rather than *olbos* for "wealth."

SUGGESTED FURTHER READING

Commentaries

Richard Caldwell's translation of and commentary on the *Theogony* (Focus, 1987) of which this an abridged version, provides an insight into the mythic and psychological bases of Hesiod's account of the gods and includes a detailed comparison with Hesiod's Near Eastern sources. Stephen Scully's forthcoming work *Hesiod's Theogony* (Oxford) includes an important consideration of Hesiod's use of language. For now see his review article in *International Journal of the Classical Tradition* 11 (2005) 424-34. The two standard, comprehensive commentaries on the main Hesiodic poems are by M. L. West, *Hesiod: Theogony* (Oxford, 1966) and *Hesiod: Works and Days* (Oxford, 1978). Both have very useful introductions largely focusing on Hesiod's ties to the Near East. In the case of the *Works and Days*, however, West is largely unimpressed with Hesiod's level of poetic ability and his commentary reflects this attitude. W. J. Verdenius has a more limited but interesting and informative commentary on the first half of the *Works and Days* (Leiden, 1985). David Tandy's translation of the *Works and Days* (Berkeley, 1997), done with an eye to the Social Sciences, contains abundant additional material, and the introduction to Glenn Most's recent Loeb edition (with Greek and English on facing pages, Cambridge, MA 2006) is excellent.

Other Works

The following include the major and most accessible of the discussions of Hesiod in, as should be clear from the various titles, his various aspects.

Burkert, Walter. *Babylon, Memphis, Persepolis: Eastern Contexts of Greek Culture.* Cambridge, MA: 2004.

Clay, Jenny Strauss, *Hesiod's Cosmos.* Cambridge: 2004.

Detienne, Marcel. *Crise agraire et attitude religieuse chez Hésiode.* Collection Latomus, Revue des Études Latines, no. 68. Brussels: 1963.

Edwards, G. P. *The Language of Hesiod in its Traditional Context.* Oxford: 1971.

Grene, David. "Hesiod: Religion and Poetry in the Works and Days." In *Radical Pluralism and Truth: David Tracy and the Hermeneutics of Religion,* ed. Werner G. Jeanrond and Jennifer L. Rike, 142-58. New York: 1991.

Jensen, Minna Skafte. "Tradition and Individuality in Hesiod's *Works and Days.*" *Classica et Mediaevalia* 27 (1966): 1-27.

Lamberton, Robert, *Hesiod.* New Haven, 1988.

Millet, Paul. "Hesiod and his World." *Cambridge Philological Society Proceedings* 209 (1983): 84-115.

Mondi, Robert. "The Ascension of Zeus and the Composition of Hesiod's *Theogony.*" *Greek, Roman, and Byzantine Studies* 25 (1984): 325-44.

_____. "Greek Mythic Thought in the Light of the Near East." In *Approaches to Greek Myth,* ed. Lowell Edmunds, 142-98. Baltimore: Johns Hopkins University Press, 1990.

Nelson, Stephanie. *God and the Land: The Metaphysics of Farming in Hesiod and Vergil.* Oxford: Oxford University Press. 1998.

Peabody, Berkeley. *The Winged Word: A Study of Ancient Greek Oral Composition as Seen Principally Through Hesiod's Works and Days.* Albany: 1975.

Pritchard, J. B.. *Ancient Near Eastern Texts,* 3rd edition with supplement (Princeton, 1969).

Pucci, Pietro. *Hesiod and the Language of Poetry.* Baltimore: 1977.

Solmsen, Friedrich. *Hesiod and Aeschylus.* Cornell Studies in Classical Philology. Ithaca: 1949.

Walcot, Peter. *Hesiod and the Near East.* Cardiff: 1966.

_____. *Greek Peasants, Ancient and Modern: A Comparison of Social and Moral Values.* Manchester: Manchester University Press, 1970.

West, M. L.. *The East Face of Helicon: West Asiatic Elements in Greek Poetry and Myth.* Oxford: 1997.

Introduction to *Theogony*

Richard Caldwell

Hesiod and the *Theogony*

The *Theogony* is a mythical account of how the Greek gods came into existence, and of the relationships and conflicts between them which led finally to a permanent divine monarchy under the rule of Zeus, the supreme god and "father of gods and men." Since many of the first gods are parts of the physical universe (e.g., earth, sky, sea), the Theogony is also an account of how the world began. It is therefore both a "theogony" (which literally means "the origin of the gods") and a cosmogony ("the origin of the world"). But its chief purpose is clearly to trace the irresistible process which resulted in the dominance of Zeus; once the world has begun and Earth and Sky have joined together as the primal couple, a series of events is set in motion which has the reign of Zeus as its inevitable and logical conclusion.

The *Theogony* was composed toward the end of the 8th century B.C. by Hesiod, a Greek farmer-poet from the region of Boeotia. Alphabetic writing had been introduced into Greece not long before and, whether Hesiod himself put the poem in writing or dictated it to someone else, the *Theogony* is possibly the oldest surviving example of Greek written literature.

We know very little about the life of Hesiod, and nothing with certainty; although fanciful legends later arose concerning him, the only relatively reliable information we have is what Hesiod says of himself in the *Theogony* or in his other surviving work, the *Works and Days,* a verse manual of ethical, mythical, and agricultural instruction. In the latter poem Hesiod says that his father left the city of Aeolian Cyme on the eastern coast of the Aegean Sea because of economic hardship and sailed across to the Greek mainland to start a new life. He settled in the village of Ascra near Mount Helicon and apparently did well enough that the inheritance he left became a matter of bitter rivalry between Hesiod and his brother Perses (WD 633-640). Hesiod himself was working as a shepherd when one day the nine Olympian Muses, divine patronesses of the arts, appeared to him on the slopes of Helicon, gave him a laurel staff, and taught him "beautiful song" (Th 22-32). The song the Muses taught Hesiod is

7

presumably the *Theogony*, and it is probably also the *Theogony* which Hesiod sang to win a prize at the funeral games of Amphidamas at Chalcis on the island of Euboea. The prize was a tripod, and Hesiod dedicated it to the Muses at the spot where they had appeared to him (WD 654-659).

How much of the *Theogony* is Hesiod's own invention is impossible to say, but it is virtually certain that he, like his contemporary Homer, was the heir to a long and rich oral tradition of poetry which included theogonic material. Some parts of this tradition seem to go back to the Neolithic origins of Indo-European myth, some to the Minoan-Mycenean world and its relations with eastern cultures, and some may be the result of specifically Boeotian development and more recent contacts between Boeotia and the Near East, perhaps through Euboea, which seems to have been a center of poetic activity.

Although we must suppose that theogonies existed in Greece before the time of Hesiod, these were oral literature and there is nothing we can know about them. Similarly, other theogonies may still have existed in Hesiod's own time and may even have been written, but no trace of them remains and we cannot know whether Hesiod's poem represents the usual view of how the world began, or whether it was merely one of several competing versions. The Greeks attributed theogonies to several early figures, some of them legendary, and Homer twice seems to recall a tradition in which Ocean and Tethys, not Sky and Earth as in Hesiod's version, were the primal couple, but the *Theogony* soon became the standard version and was for almost all later Greeks the true story of how the world began. As the historian Herodotus said three centuries later, it was Hesiod and Homer who taught the names and nature of the gods to Greece (2.53). We know that theogonies in both verse and prose continued to be written in Greece after Hesiod, but the fact of their almost complete disappearance indicates the superior authority which Hesiod's poem acquired. The best-known surviving alternatives to Hesiod's version are the peculiar theogony of the Orphic religion and the avian theogony of Aristophanes' comedy *Birds*, but these had ulterior purposes, religious parochialism in the case of the first and comedic parody in the case of the second. The predominance of Hesiod's account appears most clearly in the fact that the theogonic summary found at the beginning of the compilation of Greek myths called the Library of Apollodorus differs from Hesiod in only a few details, although it was written almost a thousand years after the *Theogony*.

It is often stated as if it were fact that Homer's *Iliad* and *Odyssey* are earlier than the *Theogony*, since the Homeric poems seem to show no knowledge of, or dependence on, the poem of Hesiod. The same argument could be used, however, to assert the priority of Hesiod, and the earliest ancient authorities seem to have believed that Hesiod was earlier than Homer. There is simply no clear evidence that either Hesiod or Homer knew the works of the other, and any resemblances between them (such as the assumption that Zeus is Cronus' son, or even shared lines and phrases) should be regarded not as borrowings or references, but as proof that both were composing within a long tradition of oral poetry which now could be preserved in writing.

It is possible, but quite unlikely, that Hesiod invented either all of the *Theogony* or none of it. The truth, as far as it can be known, is probably that he used the recent innovation of writing to compose a poem for the Chalcis competition which drew heavily on an old tradition of oral theogonic poetry, but also contained Hesiod's major and original contributions in both arrangement and content. The question of what is original and what is inherited from the poetic tradition is difficult and complicated, and ultimately impossible to resolve beyond any doubt. The matter of the Greek theogonic tradition must be left at that, even though the tradition probably extends for over a thousand years before Hesiod, for the simple reason that not a word of earlier theogonies remains.

The question of the influence of Near Eastern theogonies on Hesiod is quite different, since several of these theogonies have been preserved. Here again, however, we must distinguish between the *Theogony* of Hesiod and the Greek theogonic tradition. We can compare Near Eastern theogonies to Hesiod and note differences and similarities, but we cannot know whether Near Eastern influence affected Hesiod directly or whether it affected the Greek tradition, perhaps centuries earlier, which Hesiod inherited.

There is no doubt that there are connections between the theogonic traditions of Greece and those of the Near East. The similarities are too obvious and complex to have originated independently. Furthermore, it is generally agreed that the direction of influence went from east to west, although even this assumption cannot be stated with absolute certainty; despite the fact that the earliest Near Eastern theogonies antedate the presence itself of Greeks in Greece, it is possible that both traditions developed independently from a common pre-Bronze Age source.

The most likely conjecture is that there was a native Greek theogonic tradition as early as the first Indo-European invasion of Greece at the beginning of the 2nd millennium, and that this tradition was subject to the possibility of Near Eastern influence at virtually any time throughout (or even before) the Bronze Age, Dark Age, and early Archaic period. The two most likely occasions on which this influence might have been felt are the Minoan-Mycenean era, a time of active and extensive trade between Greece, Crete, and the Near East, and the beginning of the Archaic period with its commercial and cultural expansion. Of these two, the earlier occasion seems far more likely.

The Structure of the *Theogony*

At first glance the *Theogony* seems to be a rambling and disorderly collection of myths, genealogies, and hymns of praise. Once its plan and methods are recognized, however, the structure of the whole poem is simple and apparent. The *Theogony* is a genealogical table, or family tree, in verse. It traces the lineage of two families, who happen to be comprised of gods and goddesses, over three generations, and the inherent monotony of list after list (A married B and they begot C and D; C married D and they begot E and F, and so on) is broken up by regularly inserted expansions and digressions.

The world begins with the spontaneous emergence of four divine entities (116-120). These four — Chasm ("Chaos" in Greek), Earth (Gaia), Tartarus, and Eros — simply appear, without any source or parents, and all the other gods are ultimately descended from either Chasm or Earth, the first two gods.

The family of Chasm is smaller in extent and importance, and is made up chiefly of the fatherless personifications born to Chasm's daughter, Night or Night's daughter Strife (Eris). Hesiod's major concern is the family of Earth, not only because it eventually includes everyone and everything else but especially because it is her children and grandchildren whose couplings and battles will decide the question of divine rule in the universe. Sky (Ouranos), her son and husband, is the first sky-god to rule the world, his son Cronus is the second, and Cronus' son Zeus is the third, greatest, and last.

The genealogy of Earth's descendants is understandably complicated: children are born not only parthenogenically (i.e., from a mother alone and with no father) as in the families of Night and Strife, but also from blood or genitals or a decapitated corpse. Also, largely because of the shortage of exogamic opportunities, there is much incest, generational lines are often crossed and confused, and some figures have multiple mates. Zeus, of course, is the best example of these characteristics; in his relentless campaign to fill the world with divine, human, and mixed offspring, he marries two of his aunts, two of his sisters, and three of his cousins (he also has illegitimate children by innumerable females, but only three, his second cousin Maia and two great-granddaughters, Alcmene and Semele, are mentioned by Hesiod).

Most of the figures who appear in the genealogies are mentioned only once and play little or no part in the generational conflict which is the main theme of the *Theogony*. The chief characters in this drama, as well as the seven wives of Zeus, are represented in the following abridged genealogy:

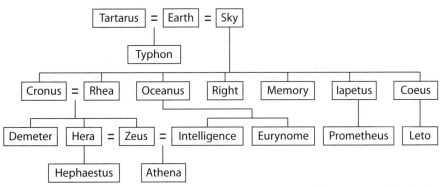

Table 1. Abridged Genealogy of the Gods

Or, if we confine ourselves to the actual succession of divine rule, the kings and queens of heaven are those of Table 2.

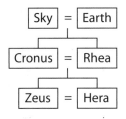

Table 2. Succession of Divine Rule

The genealogical patterns of the *Theogony* could be confusingly repetitive if it were not for their insertion in a narrative pattern which keeps our interest. This narrative, in turn, is embellished with a series of digressions which clarify the structure of the whole and furthermore allow us (and presumably also the singer, in the earlier oral tradition) to catch our breath and pause before plunging once again into the complications of who begot whom and how.

The poem begins with an invocation of the Muses, the nine daughters of Zeus and Memory (Mnemosyne) who are the titular divinities of song and were regularly called upon for inspiration and guidance at the beginning of much archaic Greek poetry. There seem, in fact, to be three separate invocations (1-35, 36-103, 104-115), each of which begins with lines that sound like a poem's beginning:

> Let us begin to sing of the Muses of Helicon
> who hold the great and holy mount of Helicon (1-2)

Hesiod, let us start from the Muses, who with singing
cheer the great mind of father Zeus in Olympus (36-37)

Greetings, children of Zeus; grant me lovely song
and praise the holy race of immortals who always are (104-105)

It is possible, but unlikely, that this tripartite division of the prologue resulted
from accretion — that is, that Hesiod (or someone else) combined separate invocations from the poetic tradition and added them to the first 35 lines (which
are obviously Hesiod's). A more plausible explanation of the repeated begin-
nings, however, would take into consideration a number of arguments in favor
of the prologue's originality and integrity. First, the three sections do not du-
plicate one another, but treat three different subjects. The first invocation tells
of the momentous vision in which the Muses granted Hesiod the gift of poetic
song; the second relates the song of the Muses, their family history, names, and
functions; the third is the introduction proper and summarizes the themes of
Hesiod's song. Second, the length and complexity of the prologue make it an
appropriate preface to a poem which may have far exceeded previous and contemporary theogonies in size and ambition. Third, the number three itself (and
its multiples) has substantial significance in the *Theogony*; to cite just some instances, there are three generations of gods (twelve Titans, six Olympians, three
children of Zeus and Hera), three Gorgons, three-headed Geryoneus, three-
headed Chimaera, three thousand sons and three thousand daughters of Ocean
and Tethys, three Cyclopes, three Hundred-Handed, three Seasons (Horae),
three Fates (Moirae), three Graces (Charites), and, of course, three times three
Muses.

The third invocation leads directly into the body of the poem, which
begins with the spontaneous appearance of Chasm, Earth, Tartarus, and Eros
(116-122). By their emergence from nothing, without source or parents, these
four are separated from everything which follows. With the appearance of Eros
(Desire), however, the situation changes and all subsequent production will be
reproduction; everything which comes into existence will have a parent, or parents, or some kind of source.

At this point Chasm and Earth begin producing offspring parthenogenically (123-132). Chasm gives birth to Erebus (Darkness) and Night, who unite
to produce their opposites, Aether (Brightness) and Day. Earth gives birth to
Sky, the Mountains, and Sea, then mates with her son Sky to produce the twelve
Titans, the three Cyclopes, and the three Hundred-Handed (133-153).

Hesiod here interrupts the genealogical presentation to tell the story of
the family of Earth and Sky (154-210). As each of their children is born, Sky
imprisons him or her in the body of their mother Earth. Finally Earth is in such

discomfort that she makes a great sickle of adamant and asks her sons to punish their father. All are too frightened to speak but Cronus, the youngest, who takes the sickle from his mother and castrates his father during his parents' sexual embrace. A number of children are born from the drops of Sky's blood which fall on the earth, and the severed penis itself, which Cronus throws into the sea, is transformed into the goddess Aphrodite.

The genealogy of the descendants of Chasm is now resumed and followed to its completion (211-232). Night, who had earlier mated with Erebus, turns to parthenogenic reproduction and bears a brood of fifteen abstractions, most of them associated with darkness and conflict. Her youngest child Strife follows her mother's example and by herself produces fifteen similar beings.

Having finished this line of descent, Hesiod returns to the children of Earth, this time to the collateral line descended not from Sky but from another son, Sea. This line is also followed to its end and consists chiefly of sea deities and hybrid monsters (233-336).

Nereus, the "old Man of the Sea," marries Doris, a daughter of the Titans Ocean and Tethys, and they are the parents of the Nereids, fifty nymphs of the sea. Thaumas marries Electra, a sister of Doris, and they produce Iris (Rainbow) and the two bird-woman Harpies.

Phorkys marries his sister Ceto and they produce a first generation of monstrous progeny.

The Gorgon Medusa's two children by Poseidon, born at the instant of her decapitation by the hero Perseus, are the winged horse Pegasus and the warrior Chrysaor. Chrysaor then marries Callirhoe, another daughter of Ocean, and their son is the three-headed Geryoneus.

Echidna, who is half-woman and half-serpent, unites with Typhon, son of Earth and Tartarus and the most fearsome monster of them all, to produce four additional monsters. Her oldest child is Orthus, the dog of Geryoneus, who is the father of two more monsters by his sister Chimaera or his mother Echidna (Hesiod's reference is ambiguous).

Hesiod now returns to the families of the Titans (337-382); since Cronus is the youngest Titan, he recounts the children of Ocean and the other older Titans before finally coming to Cronus and resuming the succession myth. The Titans Ocean, Hyperion, and Coeus marry their sisters Tethys, Theia, and Phoebe, while Crius marries his half-sister Eurybia (daughter of Earth and Sea).

After a short digression on the status of the Oceanid Styx (383-403) and a hymn in praise of the goddess Hecate (411-452), Hesiod comes to Cronus, successor to Sky as ruler of the sky, and his wife Rhea (453-506).

Cronus, who knows from his own experience that he cannot prevent being overthrown by repeating the strategy of his father Sky and keeping his children inside their mother's body, chooses instead the other alternative. He swallows each child as it is born and thus, by keeping the children in his own body rather than in that of his wife, expects to avoid the complicity of his wife in a potential rebellion. His attempt is doomed to fail, however, as his parents have predicted. When Rhea is about to give birth to Zeus, her youngest, she asks Earth and Sky for help; they send her to Crete, where Earth arranges for the nurture of Zeus without the knowledge of Cronus, while Rhea gives to Cronus a huge stone, wrapped in baby's clothing, to swallow.

When Zeus grows up he releases his uncles, the Cyclopes and Hundred-Handed, from their prison within the earth, and joins his brothers and sisters, whom Cronus has been forced to disgorge, to begin the great war between the gods and the Titans.

The succession story is now interrupted so that Hesiod can finish the genealogy of the Titans (507-520). The three members of the first Titan generation whose stories remain to be told are Iapetus, Right (Themis), and Memory, and the reason for their deferral is the involvement of them or their descendants with Zeus, who must therefore be brought into the scene. The sons of Iapetus, most notably Prometheus and Atlas, will be punished for their offenses against Zeus, and Themis and Memory will become wives of Zeus.

The reasons for Zeus' punishment of Atlas and Menoetius are unclear, but the conflict between Zeus and Prometheus is described in detail (521-569). When the gods and men met at Mecone to determine the distribution of sacrifices, Prometheus had deceived Zeus into taking the inferior portion, and Zeus retaliated by withholding from men the use of fire. Prometheus then stole fire and carried it to men in a hollow reed, whereupon Zeus punished mankind by ordering the creation of Pandora, the first woman, and sending her to men as the source of great evil (570-589). Prometheus himself was bound with inescapable chains and tortured by an eagle who ate his liver daily, until eventually Zeus allowed his son Heracles to kill the eagle and release Prometheus from his suffering. The digression ends with a misogynistic tirade against women and the admonition that no one, not even Prometheus for all his cleverness, can surpass the mind of Zeus (590-616).

The conflict between the Titans and the Olympian gods is now rejoined (617-721). The war has been raging for ten years with no end in sight until Zeus, at Earth's advice, releases the Hundred-Handed from their imprisonment. Revived by nectar and ambrosia, the food of the gods, they enter the war and the entire universe is shaken by the climactic struggle. Zeus now attacks with his lightning bolts, setting the earth and ocean on fire, and the tide of battle is turned. The Olympian gods under Zeus now rule the world, and the Titans are bound and confined in Tartarus.

In a lengthy digression (722-819), Hesiod now describes the underworld, with special emphasis on the role of the goddess/river Styx, whose primal water is the libation by which the gods swear oaths. The relevance of this long passage to the poem as a whole has often been questioned, but the logical transitions to, from, and within it are not difficult or forced. After the defeat of the Titans, the place of their punishment is appropriately described, and the portrayal of Tartarus is then expanded to include the entire underworld. The river Styx is a prominent feature of the underworld and the goddess Styx has already appeared as the oldest (777) and most eminent (361) daughter of Ocean and as an important ally of Zeus in the war against the Titans. Furthermore, she is a powerful non-Olympian goddess whose function and privileges in the underworld parallel those of Hecate, whose influence (according to Hesiod) extends throughout the world except for the underworld. Earlier in the poem both Styx and Hecate were said to have received significant gifts from Zeus (399, 412) and to have retained their previous prerogatives when Zeus came to power; now Styx is honored in her dominion, where she is invoked by the gods, as earlier Hecate had been honored and invoked by men. It seems, therefore, that Styx is the counterpart of Hecate in the underworld in the same way that Hades is the infernal counterpart of his brother Zeus.

The next episode of the *Theogony* deals with the battle between Zeus and Typhon (820-885), a conflict which recalls the earlier war between Zeus and the Titans. Tartarus, whose description began the previous section, appears again in two different forms, as the father of Typhon and as the place where Typhon will be punished alongside the Titans. Again the world is shaken to its foundations and the earth is set on fire by the terrible struggle, and again Zeus is victorious. With this triumph the rule of Zeus is officially established; he determines the positions of the other gods and then turns to the business of procreation, his principal concern henceforth.

Hesiod now lists the seven goddesses who become wives of Zeus and the offspring who result from these unions (886-923). Zeus first marries the Oceanid Metis (Intelligence), but when she is about to give birth to Athena, Zeus learns that her second child is fated to replace him as king of gods and men. Unlike Cronus, who swallowed his children, Zeus deals with the potential threat by swallowing his wife.

The second wife of Zeus is his aunt Right (Themis), who bears the three Seasons and the three Fates. She is followed by the Oceanid Eurynome, who produces a third triad, the Graces. The fourth wife is Zeus' sister Demeter, and their daughter Persephone will become the wife of Hades. Next is another aunt,

Memory, the mother of the nine Muses. Sixth is Leto, daughter of the Titans Coeus and Phoebe and mother of Apollo and Artemis.

Zeus' seventh and final wife is his sister Hera, and their children are Youth (Hebe), Ares, and Eileithyia, goddess of childbirth. At this point Zeus gives birth from his head to the goddess Athena, with whom Intelligence had been pregnant when he swallowed her. Angered by the independent procreation practiced by her husband, Hera now produces Hephaestus parthenogenically (927-929).

The last section of the *Theogony* is a series of brief genealogical mentions beginning with Zeus' brother Poseidon (his other brother Hades has no children) and Zeus' son Ares, and going on to various unions involving gods (including Zeus) and then goddesses (930-1020). The order of presentation is based on a patriarchal hierarchy, according to the divinity of father, children, and finally mother. The entire passage forms a transition to a lost genealogical poem attributed to Hesiod, the *Catalogue of Women*, which told of families descended from the unions of mortal women with gods. The last two lines of our *Theogony* introduce the subject of the *Catalogue*; the last 100 or so lines of the *Theogony*, as well as the *Catalogue* whose fragments have survived, were written by an imitator of Hesiod, perhaps during the 6th century.

After Hesiod the origin of the gods seems to have held much less interest for Greek myth than mortal heroes and the relationships of heroes with one another and with the gods. The divine world becomes a kind of background (sometimes, as in the *Iliad* and certain tragedies, a background with a mirrored surface) to the world of heroes and their adventures. This relative lack of interest in theogonic matters may help answer two questions in regard to the *Theogony*. First, the virtually unchallenged authority of Hesiod may be due not only to the date at which he wrote (that is, to his position as both the last in a long oral tradition and the first theogony-poet to commit his poem to writing), but also to the shift in attention and emphasis from divine to primarily human matters (a shift which took place long before either Hesiod or Homer). Second, the apparently excessive number of lines spent on such matters as the description of the underworld, the catalogues of nymphs and monsters, the praise of the Muses, Styx, and Hecate, and the complaint against women (which together make up half of the poem) may be due to this shift and to the simple fact that these were not the usual subjects of mythology. The *Theogony* is basically a logistical poem, and its purpose is setting the pieces of divine machinery in place and in order. The inherent tediousness of this project needs to be relieved, but the means by which this relief is accomplished is hymnic or descriptive material rather than episodes from heroic myth. The chief characteristic of all the digressions from the main business of the poem (the genealogies and the succession story) is their static nature. Catalogue, hymn, description, and diatribe are essentially motionless elements which divide into separate segments the chronological and unilinear movement of genealogy and generational conflict.

This does not mean, however, that the digressions are irrelevant to the larger purpose of the poem. Nymphs and monsters are often as necessary as the gods themselves in the setting and plots of heroic myth, and it is the *Theogony* which provides this setting. The underworld description is significant not only because the underworld is where most of the chief actors in the succession drama are lodged either temporarily or permanently, but also because it has an inevitable, if potential, importance for the lives of the poem's human audience (who may never see Olympus, but will certainly spend time in the underworld). The wish to establish a human contact is understandable in a poem specifically concerned with the non-human world, and may also explain the attention given to the Muses, Styx, and Hecate; they are divinities who, in Hesiod's view, directly affect human life and death.

The same is true of the long central panel of the poem, the two-part digression on Prometheus and Pandora. Both phases of the conflict between Prometheus and Zeus, the sacrificial dispute and the theft of fire, are concerned with crucial factors in human existence, the first with mankind's role in its relationship with the gods, and the second with the institution and value of civilization itself. The final outcome of this conflict, the creation of Pandora, turns a conflict between deities into a central fact of human life, the battle of the sexes. The ambivalence of the gods themselves, their often quixotic alternation between benevolence and destructiveness, is reflected in the "lovely evil" (585) of woman.

We may note in passing that the same explicit use of mythical digressions to characterize human life is found in the *Works and Days*. Here there are two such digressions, related one after another at the beginning of the poem: the first tells the story of Prometheus and Pandora, a bit differently than the *Theogony* version, and the second is the myth of the Five Ages through which mankind has descended. The aim of both digressions is to trace the background and causes of the present human situation, to explain the grim conditions of life (in Hesiod's pessimistic view) in terms of mythical antecedents. If life is full of troubles, evil, and disease, it is because of Pandora (and, ultimately, Prometheus and Zeus); and if mankind has never-ending labor and grief, with strife and violence as the ordinary state of human relationships, this is because the men of Hesiod's time are an "iron race," living in the last and worst of the five mythical ages.

Before we leave the subject of the *Theogony*'s structure there is one matter, alluded to earlier, which should now be treated in greater detail: the inevitable, logically necessary process which leads from the union of Earth and Sky to the permanent sovereignty of Zeus.

It will be helpful first to summarize the succession myth. Earth marries her son Sky and they have eighteen children, whom Sky does not allow to emerge from their mother's body. Earth, distressed by this, somehow gives her youngest son Cronus an adamantine sickle, which he uses to castrate his father during the act of intercourse. Cronus now releases at least eleven of his brothers and sisters, the Titans, and becomes king of the gods; whether he also releases the three Cyclopes and three Hundred-Handed, and then re-confines them, is unclear in Hesiod's text. Cronus marries his sister Rhea, an earth-goddess like her mother, and they have six children, the first generation of Olympian gods. However, as each of his children is born, Cronus swallows him or her. Finally, when Rhea is about to give birth to Zeus, she gives Cronus a stone, disguised as a baby, to swallow, and Zeus is secretly born and raised in Crete. When he has grown to maturity, Zeus leads and wins a great war against his father and the other Titans, aided by the released Cyclopes and Hundred-Handed and by his fellow Olympians, whom Cronus has been forced to disgorge through a trick of Earth. Zeus now becomes the third king of the world and marries first the Oceanid nymph Intelligence (Metis). While she is pregnant with Athena, Zeus learns from his grandparents that Intelligence' second child is fated to be a son who will rule over gods and men. Zeus prevents the birth of this child by swallowing Intelligence, gives birth to Athena from his own head, and secures his permanent reign.

We may begin with an obvious question: why does Sky confine his children in their mother's body? His son Cronus and grandson Zeus will naturally take steps to prevent being overthrown, because they know what happened to their predecessors, but what prior knowledge could Sky possibly have which might cause him to suspect that one of his children will try to usurp his position? Hesiod says merely that Sky "hated" his sons because they were "most terrible" (155), but how could he know this if the children are not even allowed to be born? Perhaps Sky heard the children misbehaving inside their mother — there is actually a parallel for this in a Babylonian myth — but a more reasonable explanation is available. Gods, like children, tend to rely on their own past experiences to determine their present behavior, and Sky has a good reason from his past to fear his children. This reason is the fact that he married his mother; if Sky did this (and, at this early point of cosmic history, he knows of no alternate behavior), his children will want to do the same, and therefore he must suppress them. Now Sky must make a decision. His children, being immortal, cannot be killed, but must be imprisoned, and there are only two possible locations: either in the sky (that is, in himself) or in the earth (that is, in their mother). Sky chooses the latter, and it is the wrong choice; his son Cronus, thanks to the intervention and complicity of Earth, castrates and replaces his father.

Cronus now faces a similar situation. If he does not renounce sexual activity (which would be equivalent to renouncing his position as paternal sky-god), he must arrange that his sons will not do to him the same thing he did to his father. The decision he takes is clearly derived from his memory of what had happened to Sky and from his intention to avoid a similar fate by adopting a different strategy. In order to prevent his sons from overthrowing him, he thinks, he cannot keep them in their mother's body, but must keep mother and sons separate as well as suppressing the sons themselves. Therefore Cronus chooses the strategy Sky had rejected, and puts his children into his own body rather than into their mother's.

The choice of Cronus is logically quite simple. Since he cannot kill his children and does not want to adopt the failed strategy of Sky, the only option remaining — an obvious but significant emendation of Sky's tactic — is to imprison either his children or his wife in the other parental body, in himself rather than in Rhea. Cronus must swallow either his children or his wife, and he chooses the former presumably because the alternative would not only leave his children running free but also would deprive him of his sexual partner. In fact, he would have to swallow his wife immediately upon the birth of their first child (and, I imagine, hope that this first child is a daughter).

The oracular warning given to Cronus by his parents (463-464) is therefore superfluous. It merely reminds him of his own experience and tells him nothing new, except that he will make the wrong choice. Zeus in turn will be faced with the same situation and the same choices, but he will choose correctly; that is, he will swallow his wife instead of his children. By electing this strategy (which involves no great thought, since it is the only remaining alternative), Zeus will establish himself as the most notable exception to the underlying law of myth, as well as of life, that fathers are destined to be replaced by their sons, and he will exemplify the male wish that what he wanted to do to his father will not be done to him in turn.

Therefore we know, even before we are told, that Zeus will have to swallow a wife. He has learned from the fates of Sky and Cronus that to put his children in either his wife's body or his own is not a satisfactory solution, and he also realizes that the real enemy is not so much the children as the wife. Zeus must either repeat the mistake of his ancestors (which he cannot do, or someone else would now be ruling the sky), or he must put his wife, not his children, inside himself. There is no other alternative.

Thus the Hesiodic tradition created a succession myth of striking psychological logic. This primal story of generational rivalry, marital conflict, and maternal preference is reduced to a series of clear-cut either/or choices which lead inevitably to the accession of Zeus as the greatest and permanent sky-god. The strict logic of the process and the certainty of its conclusion are embellished by several imaginative hints of Zeus' final victory. For example, even while the war between Zeus and the Titans is in progress, Hesiod pauses to tell the story of Zeus' triumph over Prometheus. And in this story Hesiod almost certainly alters the tradition he had received, which probably told of Zeus really being deceived by Prometheus and choosing the wrong portion. In the Theogony, however, Hesiod substitutes a version in which Zeus—who will later, on a more important occasion, make the correct and only decision—now merely pretends to choose wrongly.

Richard Caldwell

Theogony

[Prologue]

Let us begin to sing of the Muses of Helicon,[1]
who hold the great and holy mount of Helicon,
and dance on tender feet round the violet spring
and the altar of Cronus' mighty son.
Having washed their soft skin in Permessus'   5
spring, or Hippocrene, or holy Olmeius,[2]
on Helicon's summit they lead the fair
dances arousing longing, with rapid steps.
Setting out from there, concealed by air,
they walk at night, chanting their fair song,   10
singing of aegis-bearing Zeus[3] and mistress Hera
of Argos, who walks in golden sandals, and
aegis-bearing Zeus' daughter, bright-eyed Athena,
and Phoebus Apollo and archeress Artemis,

---

1   The Muses invoked by Hesiod are the divine patronesses of song and singers. It
    was a common practice in early Greek poetry to begin a recitation with an appeal
    to them (or to one of them) for inspiration and guidance. Hesiod introduces his
    song with a hymn to the Muses because they are more than a poetic convention
    to him; they actually appeared to him and made him a singer (22-33), and they
    commanded him to sing first of themselves. Mount Helicon is the highest
    mountain of Boeotia, about halfway between Thebes and Delphi. The town of
    Ascra on its slopes was the home of Hesiod; according to Pausanias (9.29.1-2)
    Ascra was founded by the Aloadae (two gigantic children who tried to take over
    Olympus), and they also started a cult of the Muses on Helicon. There may have
    been a cult of Zeus on Helicon, as the presence of an altar implies.

2   The Permessus is a stream of Helicon, and the Olmeius is a nearby river into which
    it flowed. Hippocrene, a spring high on Helicon, was later said to have been created
    by a kick of the hoof of the winged horse Pegasus; the name means "spring of the
    horse."

3   Zeus' descriptive epithet "Aegiochos" is usually translated "aegis-bearing" and
    thought to refer to the aegis, a goat-skin emblem made by Hephaestus for Zeus,
    who uses it to frighten enemies and create thunder-storms.

and Poseidon earth-embracer, earth-shaker,[4]   15
and revered Right (Themis)[5] and glancing Aphrodite,
and gold-crowned Youth (Hebe) and lovely Dione,
Leto, Iapetus, and crooked-minded Cronus,[6]
Dawn, great Sun (Helius), and bright Moon (Selene)
Earth (Gaia), great Ocean, and black Night, and   20
the holy race of other immortals who always are.
      Once they taught Hesiod beautiful song
as he watched his sheep under holy Helicon;
this is the first speech the goddesses spoke to me,
the Olympian Muses, daughters of aegis-bearing Zeus:[7]   25
      "Rustic shepherds, evil oafs, nothing but bellies,
we know how to say many lies as if they were true,[8]
and when we want, we know how to speak the truth."
      This is what the prompt-voiced daughters of great Zeus said;
they picked and gave me a staff, a branch of strong laurel,[9]   30
a fine one, and breathed into me a voice
divine, to celebrate what will be and what was.

---

4   Poseidon is called "earth-embracer" because he is a sea-god, and the ocean was
     regarded by the gods as a circular river which surrounded the earth.

5   Right (Themis) is a Titan goddess (135) and Zeus' second wife (901).

6   Hebe (Youth) is a daughter of Zeus and Hera (922). Dione is a daughter of Ocean
     in the *Theogony* (353), but Homer and some other sources call her the mother of
     Aphrodite; her name is a feminine form of "Zeus." Leto is a daughter of the Titans
     Coeus and Phoebe (404-406) and Zeus' sixth wife (918); their children are Apollo
     and Artemis (919). Iapetus is a Titan (134) and the father of Prometheus (510).

7   The "Olympian" Muses are the same as the "Heliconian" Muses in 1; they are
     called Heliconian because Helicon is one of their favorite places and a site of their
     cult, and Olympian because they sing to and of their father Zeus, whose home is
     Olympus.

8   The lies which have the appearance of truth may refer to variants and
     contradictions in the theogonic traditions which Hesiod knew.

9   To hold a staff, in early Greek literature, is to have the authority to speak; staffs are
     held by kings, priests, prophets, heralds, and speakers in the Homeric assembly of
     chieftains. Professional singers after the time of Hesiod often carried a laurel wand,
     and an ancient commentator claimed that Hesiod invented this practice (no doubt
     using this passage as his evidence). The laurel is associated with Apollo and with
     oracles and prophecy; it is therefore fitting for singers also, since singers and prophets
     in ancient Greece shared a calling and knowledge not available to ordinary mortals.
     There were other concrete signs (blindness, for example) which, at least in myth and
     legend, characterize both singers and prophets as possessors of arcane knowledge.

They told me to sing the race of the blessed who always are,
but always to sing of themselves first and also last.
But what is this of oak or rock to me?[10]   35
            Hesiod, let us start from the Muses, who with singing
cheer the great mind of father Zeus in Olympus,[11]
telling things that are and will be and were before,
with harmonized voice; the unbroken song flows
sweet from their lips; the father's house rejoices,   40
the house of loud-sounding Zeus,[12] as the delicate voice
of the goddesses spreads, the peaks of snowy Olympus echo,
and the homes of the immortals; with ambrosial voice
they celebrate in song[13] first the revered race of gods
from the beginning, whom Earth and wide Sky begot,   45
and those born from them, the gods, givers of good;
and second of Zeus, the father of gods and men,
[the goddesses sing, beginning and ending the song]
how he is best of gods and greatest in strength;
next, singing of the race of men and mighty Giants   50
they cheer the mind of Zeus in Olympus, themselves
the Muses of Olympus, daughters of aegis-bearing Zeus.
Memory (Mnemosyne), who rules the hills of Eleuther, having lain
with the father, Cronus' son, in Pieria, bore them to be
a forgetting of evils and a respite from cares.[14]   55

---

10   This puzzling line must be a proverb of some kind. The meaning may be "Why
      do I speak further of incredible things?" (i.e., the epiphany of the Muses), but this
      cannot be demonstrated. At any rate, the verse is an indication that one topic is
      ending and another is about to begin.

11   Having told of his own relationship with the Muses, Hesiod now starts over. This
      second part of his prologue is much more like the standard hymn to a divinity,
      relating the Muses' function and situation among the gods (37-74), the details
      of their parentage and birth (53-62), their names (75-79), and their functions in
      regard to mortals (80-103).

12   Zeus is "loud-sounding" because he is a thunder-, lightning-, and storm-god.

13   The song of the Muses recapitulates the themes of the *Theogony* and its sequel, the
      Catalogue of Women: the first gods and the Titans (44-45), the Olympian gods (46),
      Zeus (47, 49), mortals (50).

14   Memory (Mnemosyne), the mother of the Muses is most important to a poet whose
      tradition is entirely or largely orally transmitted. Eleuther is on Mount Cithaeron,
      another Boeotian mountain which may have been the site of a cult of the Muses, as
      well as the place where the infant Oedipus was exposed and where Heracles killed

For wise Zeus lay with her nine nights[15]
apart from the immortals, going up to the holy bed;
but when a year went by, and the seasons turned round,
as months waned, and many days were completed,
she bore nine like-minded daughters, in whose   60
breasts and spirit song is the only care,
just below the summit of snowy Olympus. There
are their polished dance-floors and lovely houses;
next to them the Graces and Longing have homes
in festivity; chanting from their lips a lovely song,   65
they sing, and celebrate the customs and noble ways of
all the immortals, chanting a most lovely song.
Then they went to Olympus, rapt in the lovely air,
the ambrosial song; the black earth echoed round
to their singing, and a lovely beat arose under their   70
feet as they went to their father; he was ruling the
sky as king, holding the thunder and fiery lightning-bolt himself,
having the victory from his father Cronus by strength; in right detail
he dealt laws and appointed honors to the immortals.
These things the Muses sang, who hold Olympian homes,   75
nine daughters begotten by great Zeus,
Clio the Glorifying, Euterpe the Well Delighting,
Thalia the Festive, and Melpomene the Singing One,
Terpsichore, Delighting in Dance, Erato, the Lovely,
Polymnia the Many Hymning, Ourania the Heavenly,
and Calliope the Beautiful Voiced, most eminent of all,
for she is companion of revered kings.[16]   80

---

a monstrous lion. Pieria, the area north of Mount Olympus in Thessaly, was well-known in antiquity for its cult of the Muses, as *Works and Days* 1.

15   The intercourse of Zeus and Memory lasts for nine nights because she will bear nine children. Somewhat similarly, Zeus is said to have enjoyed the night he spent with Alcmene so much that he extended the night to three times its normal length (Apollodorus 2.4.8), and this inordinate amount of time was responsible for the great strength of Heracles, the child Alcmene conceived (Diodoros 4.9).

16   The number and names of the nine Muses may have been invented by Hesiod. There is of course no way to prove this, but a reason to suspect that the names occur here for the first time is the fact that the names reflect words and phrases earlier used by Hesiod (West, *Theogony*, 180-181). It was not until late Roman times that individual Muses were given separate authority for different arts. A modern "museum" is a "place of the Muses" (*mouseion*), and in ancient Greece philosophers

Whomever of kings, favored by Zeus, the daughters
of great Zeus honor and see being born,
they pour sweet dew on his tongue, and
from his lips flow honeyed words; his people
all look to him as he decides issues with   85
straight judgments; making speeches unerringly he
quickly and wisely ends even a great quarrel;
this is why there are sensible kings, since
they secure works of restitution for the wronged in
assembly and easily, persuading by soft words;   90
going to assembly, they pray to him as to a god,
with supplicant reverence; in assembly he is pre-eminent.
Such is the holy gift of the Muses to men.
For from the Muses and far-shooting Apollo
are men on the land who sing and play the harp,   95
but kings are from Zeus; he prospers, whom the
Muses love; a sweet voice flows from his lips.
For if one has grief in his newly-vexed spirit, and
his heart is withered in sorrow, and then a bard,
the Muses' servant, sings the fame of former men   100
and the blessed gods who hold Olympus, soon
he forgets his mind's burden and remembers none of
his cares; quickly the goddesses' gifts divert him.
         Greetings, children of Zeus; grant me lovely song,[17]
and celebrate the holy race of immortals who always are,   105
who were born from Earth and starry Sky,
and from dark Night, and those salty Sea raised.
Tell how at first gods and earth came to be,
and rivers and vast sea, violent in surge,
and shining stars and the wide sky above,   110
[and the gods born from them, givers of good]
how they divided their wealth and allotted honors
and how first they held valed Olympus.
Tell me these things, Muses with Olympian homes,

(such as Plato and Aristotle) and scholars put their schools under the sponsorship
of the Muses.

17   Again Hesiod seems to start over. This section describes the main genealogical
      concerns of his poem, and also suggests his main purpose, to depict the
      establishment of a permanent divine hierarchy on Olympus (112-113).

from the first, say which of them first came to be.   115

[First Beings]

First of all Chasm (Chaos)[18] came into being; but next
wide-breasted Earth, always safe foundation of all
immortals who possess the peaks of snowy Olympus,[19]
and dim Tartarus[20] in a nook of the wide-pathed land,
and Eros,[21] most beautiful among the immortal gods,   120
limb-weakener, who masters the mind and sensible counsel
in the breasts of all gods and all men.
    From Chasm were born Erebus (Darkness) and black Night;
from Night were born Aether (Brightness) and Day,
whom she conceived and bore, joined in love with Erebus.   125
Earth first bore a child equal to herself,
starry Sky (Ouranos), to cover her all over, and
to be an always safe home for the blessed gods.
She bore the high Mountains, pleasing homes of divine
nymphs, who dwell in the valed mountains.   130
She also bore the barren Sea,[22] violent in surge,
without love's union; but next

---

18   The primary meaning of the Greek word "chaos" is not disorder or confusion, but
      rather an opening or gap. Related to the verb "chasko" (open, yawn, gape), "chaos"
      signifies a void, an abyss, infinite space and darkness, unformed matter. The concept
      of this primordial Chasm is reminiscent of the boundless and featureless watery
      waste called Nun in Egyptian cosmogony and the formless void and abyss of Genesis.

19   Earth is the primal mother from whom almost all of subsequent creation is
      descended. In virtually all cosmogonies (with the topographically determined
      exception of the Egyptian) Earth is the primordial maternal symbol, and in Greek
      myth she plays an especially important role as mother and wife of Heaven, mother
      of the Titans, and grandmother of Zeus and the first generation of Olympian gods.

20   Tartarus is the lowest part of the underworld, and since the underworld is
      everything below the surface of the earth, Tartarus seems to be the lowest part
      of Earth. Like many cosmogonic phenomena, Tartarus is both a place and also a
      (barely) anthropomorphized being, who mates and produces offspring but has no
      personality or career.

21   Eros is a creative principle of Desire in the universe; his appearance is the necessary
      condition separating the first stage of the world from all later development. After
      Eros comes into existence, all creation will be procreation.

22   Earth's final parthenogenic son is Sea (Pontus), by whom she will later produce
      children (233-239). The distinction between Sea and Ocean is based on the
      identification of Ocean as a river which encircled the earth.

she lay with Sky and bore deep-whirling Ocean,
and Coeus and Crius and Hyperion and Iapetus,
and Theia and Rhea and Right and Memory   135
and gold-crowned Phoebe and lovely Tethys.
After them was born the youngest, crooked-minded Cronus,[23]
most terrible of children; he hated his lusting father.
        Next she bore the Cyclopes with over-proud heart,
Brontes the Thunderer and Steropes, Lightening, and hard-hearted   140
Arges the Bright, who gave Zeus thunder and made the lightning-bolt.[24]
They were like the gods in everything else,
but a single eye was in the middle of their foreheads;
they were given the name Cyclopes, the Circle-eyed, because
one round eye was in their foreheads;   145
strength, force, and skill were in their works.
Next others were born from Earth and Sky,
three great and mighty sons, unspeakable
Cottus and Briareus and Gyges, rash children.
From their shoulders shot a hundred arms   150
unimaginable, and fifty heads on the shoulders
of each grew over their strong bodies;
great and mighty strength was in their huge shape.

23   The twelve children here named will be called the Titans by their father Heaven in
      207.
24   These Cyclopes are sometimes called the "ouranian" Cyclopes for their father
      Ouranos or Sky; later Hephaestus will replace them as armorer of the gods, with
      the Cyclopes as his assistants.

[The Castration of Sky]

> For all who were born from Earth and Sky were the
> most terrible of children, and their father hated them   155
> from the first; when any of them first would be born,
> he would hide them all away, and not let them come up
> to the light, in a dark hole of Earth; the evil deed
> pleased Sky. But she, vast Earth, groaned within
> from the strain, and planned an evil deceitful craft.   160
> Quick she made the element of grey adamant,
> made a great sickle,[25] and advised her sons,
> speaking encouragingly, while hurt in her heart:
>   "Children of me and a wicked father, if you are willing
> to obey, we may punish the evil outrage of your   165
> father; since he first planned unseemly deeds."
> She said this, but fear seized them all and none of them
> spoke. But great and crooked-minded Cronus was brave, and
> quickly answered with speech to his dear mother:
>   "Mother, I would undertake and do this task,   170
> since I have no respect for our father
> unspeakable; since he first planned unseemly deeds."
>   He spoke and vast Earth was greatly pleased in her mind.
> She placed and hid him in ambush, and put in his hands
> a sickle with jagged teeth, and revealed the whole trick.   175
> Great Sky came, bringing on night,[26] and upon Earth
> he lay, longing for love and fully extended;
> his son, from ambush, reached out with his left hand
> and with his right hand took the huge sickle,
> long with jagged teeth, and quickly severed   180
> his own father's genitals, and threw them to fall
> behind; they did not fall from his hand without result,
> for all the bloody drops which spurted were
> received by Earth; as the year revolved,
> she bore the strong Furies (Erinyes) and great Giants,   185
> shining in armor, holding long spears in their hands,

---

25   Adamant is a mythical element, hardest of all metals; its name means
      "unconquerable." A sickle is the weapon often used to fight monsters. Perseus uses
      a sickle to decapitate the Gorgon Medusa, and Iolaus uses a sickle to help Heracles
      against the monstrous Hydra during Heracles' second labor.

26   Sky's embrace of Earth is so close it blots out the light, thus "bringing on night."

and the nymphs called Meliae, Ash Tree nymphs, on the endless earth. [27]
As soon as he cut off the genitals with adamant,
he threw them from land into the turbulent sea;
they were carried over the sea a long time, and white   190
foam arose from the immortal flesh; within a girl
grew; first she came to holy Cythera, and
next she came to wave-washed Cyprus.
A revered and beautiful goddess emerged, and
grass grew under her supple feet. Aphrodite   195
[foam-born goddess and well-crowned Cytherea]
gods and men name her, since in foam she grew;
and Cytherea, since she landed at Cythera;
and Cyprogenea, since she was born in wave-beat Cyprus;
and "Philommeides," since she appeared from the genitals. [28]   200
Eros accompanied her, and fair Longing followed,
when first she was born and went to join the gods.
She has such honor from the first, and this is her
portion among men and immortal gods:
maidens' whispers and smiles and deceptions,   205
sweet pleasure and sexual love and tenderness.
      Great Sky, their father, called his sons Titans, or Strainers, [29]
quarreling with the sons whom he himself begot;
he said they strained in wickedness to do a deed
of great evil, but there would be revenge afterwards.   210

---

27   The Furies are mythical spirits of retributive vengeance who punish those crimes,
      especially within the family, which threaten the traditional structures of home
      and society. Their particular concern with the crimes of children against parents
      may be seen in their pursuit of the mythical matricide Orestes. The nymphs called
      Meliae are properly "ash-tree" nymphs; the Greek word for ash-trees is *meliae* also.
      Why they are mentioned here, or born in this way, is unclear and may reflect a local
      aetiological myth.

28   The birth of Aphrodite from the castration of Sky is not so bizarre or at least so
      incongruous as it may seem. Just as Athena, goddess of wisdom, will be born from
      the head of Zeus, now the goddess of sexual desire is born from a god's genitals.
      The names Cythereia and Cyprogenes, as Hesiod says, are due to her associations
      with the islands Cythera and Cyprus, which were early and famous centers of
      the worship of Aphrodite. Philommeides (laughter-loving) is an early epithet of
      Aphrodite (*Iliad* 3.424, *Odyssey* 8.362, *Th* 989). Hesiod's pun plays on the similarity
      in pronunciation between *meid* (laughter) and *med* (genitals).

29   Hesiod derives the name Titans from the verb *titaino* (strain); there is also a
      secondary connection with *tisis* (revenge).

[The Children of Night]

Night bore hateful Fate and black Doom and
Death, she bore Sleep and the tribe of Dreams.[30]
Next Blame and painful Trouble were born to
the dark goddess Night, though she lay with no one,
and the Hesperides who keep, beyond famous Ocean,   215
the beautiful gold apples and the fruit-bearing trees;
and she bore the Fates and pitiless Dooms,
[Clotho the Spinner and Lachesis the Allotter and Atropos the Unbending,
who give to mortals at birth both good and evil to have]
who pursue the sins of men and gods;   220
the goddesses never end their terrible anger
until they inflict evil on anyone who sins.[31]
And deadly Night bore Nemesis (Retribution),[32] a plague to mortal
men; after her she bore Deceit and Fondness
and painful Old Age and strong-hearted Strife.[33]   225

---

30   Before relating the families of the Titans, Hesiod returns to the first generation
      and completes the story of the descendants of Night (211-232) and of Earth and
      her son Sea (233-336). All the children of Night are thematically associated with
      her in some way; they occur at night (e.g., Dreams, Fondness) or they are dark
      and terrible (e.g., Death, Deceit, Strife) like "dark" (214) and "deadly" (223) Night
      herself. The Hesperides are beautiful nymphs who, along with Atlas (517-520) and a
      monstrous serpent (334-335), guard the tree of golden apples in a marvelous garden
      somewhere in the imaginary world at the ends of the earth.

31   Hesiod later calls the Fates (Moirai) the daughters of Zeus and Right (Themis) (904),
      and gives them the names which they traditionally have, but the names seem here to
      be assigned to the Dooms (Keres). They must, however, belong to the Fates; 218-219
      are almost identical to a later description of the Fates (905-906) and may have been
      inserted here from the later passage by an editor or commentator who wanted to
      balance the description of the Dooms. The Fates and Dooms are plural forms of the
      singular Fate and Doom in 211; both represent the destined end of life.

32   The special role of Nemesis (Retribution) is to punish excess, whether of good or of
      evil, and in this leveling function she is the agent of Zeus, who "crushes the strong,"
      "lowers the high," and "withers the proud" (WD 5-7). Nemesis represents the
      fundamental Greek conception that anyone who rises too high exposes himself to
      the envy and vengeance of the gods. The famous shrine of Nemesis near Marathon
      in Attica contained a statue of the goddess which the sculptor Phidias made from a
      block of Parian marble; the invading Persians had brought the marble, intending to
      set up a trophy after they defeated the Athenians.

33   Strife (Eris) is the spirit of enmity and conflict who "advances evil war and battle"
      (WD 14), and who used a golden apple to start a conflict between three goddesses

And hateful Strife bore painful Toil,
Lethe (Forgetfulness) and Famine and tearful Pains,
Battles, Fighting, Murders, and Slayings of Men;
Quarrels, Lies, Words (Logoi), and Contentious Words,
Ill-governance and Ruin (Atê), near one another,   230
and Oath, who most afflicts men on earth,
when anyone willingly swears a false oath.[34]

[The Children of Sea and Earth, the Nereids]

Sea begot Nereus, truthful and never false,
eldest of his children; he is called the Old Man
since he is infallible and gentle; what is lawful   235
he remembers, and he knows just and gentle thoughts.[35]
Then he begot great Thaumas and proud Phorcys,
from union with Earth, and fair-cheeked Ceto, and
Eurybia, who has in her breast a heart of adamant.[36]

    To Nereus were born numerous divine children   240
in the barren sea; their mother was fair-haired Doris,
daughter of Ocean, the full-circling river:
Protho, Eucrante, Sao, Amphitrite,
Eudora, Thetis, Galene, and Glauce,
Cymothoe, swift Speio, lovely Festivity,   245
Pasithea, Erato, and rose-armed Eunice,
graceful Melite, Eulimene, Agaue,
Doto, Proto, Pherusa, and Dynamene,

---

which led to the Trojan War. In the *Works and Days* Hesiod reconsiders and says that
she has an older sister, also named Strife, who personifies healthy competition (11-26).

34   Ruin (atê) is doom resulting from delusion or misguided thinking. Homer, who
calls her the daughter of Zeus, tells how she deceived her father and was banished
from Olympus (*Iliad* 19. 85-138). Oath is a negative concept because he represents
the punishment one promises to undergo if an oath is false (e.g., "if I am lying [or
do not do what I say], may I be punished").

35   Nereus is often called the "Old Man of the Sea" or simply the "Old Man". The
metamorphic power of the sea-gods is often connected with their prophetic ability:
Proteus turns into a lion, serpent, leopard, boar, water, and a tree in his effort to avoid
Menelaus' questions about the future (*Odyssey* 4. 456-458); Nereus changes into
water and fire before telling Heracles the directions to the garden of the Hesperides.

36   Thaumas, Phorcys, and Ceto will be the parents of monstrous and marvelous
offspring, and their names hint at this. "Thauma" means "marvel," "ketos" means
"whale" or "sea-monster," and "phoke" resembles the Greek word for "seal".

Nesaia, Actaea, and Protomedea,
Doris and Panope and shapely Galateia,   250
lovely Hippothoe, rose-armed Hipponoe,
Cymodoce, who easily calms waves on the windy
sea and the blowing of windy gales,
with Cymatolege and fine-ankled Amphitrite,
and Cymo, Eione, and well-crowned Halimede,   255
Glauconome, who loves smiles, and Sea-going,
Leagora and Euagora and Laomedea,
Poulynoe and Autonoe and Lysianassa,
Euarne of lovely shape and blameless form,
Psamathe of graceful body, divine Menippe,   260
Neso, Eupompe, Themisto, and Pronoe, and
Nemertes the Infallible, who has the mind of her immortal father.
These were the daughters of blameless Nereus:
fifty girls, skilled in blameless works.[37]

---

37   The fifty Nereid nymphs are representations of the beautiful and positive aspects of
      the sea and appear in myth usually as attractive spectators. Nereids of individual
      significance are Amphitrite (243, the wife of Poseidon at 930) and Thetis (244), the
      most famous Nereid. When Zeus learns that she is fated to bear a son who will be
      greater than his father, he forces her to marry the mortal Peleus. The son of Thetis
      and Peleus is Achilles, and Thetis plays a major role in the *Iliad* as protector and
      advisor of her son.

[Birth of the Monsters]

Thaumas married deep-flowing Ocean's 265
daughter Electra; she bore swift Iris the Rainbow
and the fair-haired Harpies, Aello and Ocypete,
who fly as the birds and gusts of winds
on swift wings, rushing high in the air.[38]
Ceto bore to Phorcys the fair-cheeked hags, 270
grey from birth, who are called the Graeae[39]
by immortal gods and men who go on earth,
fine-robed Pemphredo and saffron-robed Enyo,
and the Gorgons,[40] who live beyond famous Ocean,
at the limit toward Night, with the clear-voiced 275
Hesperides, Sthenno, Euryale, and unlucky Medusa;
she was mortal, but they were immortal and ageless,
both of them; the Dark-Haired god, Poseidon, lay with her
in a soft meadow and flowers of spring.
And when Perseus cut off her head, out 280
jumped great Chrysaor, the Golden Sworded and the horse Pegasus,
who has this name since by the springs (*pegai*) of Ocean
he was born, and the other holds a gold sword in his hands;

38 Iris is the personification of the rainbow and, since the rainbow seems to connect sky
and earth, she is a messenger between gods and men. The Harpies are storm-wind
spirits. They appear on grave stones carrying the souls of the dead, and are said to
have carried off the daughters of Pandareus (*Odyssey* 20.77). To be "carried away by
the stormwinds" or "by the Harpies" seems to mean "to disappear" or "to die."

39 The two Graeae have in later accounts a third sister, usually named Deino
(Apollodorus 2.4.2). According to Apollodorus, they have only one eye and one
tooth between them, which they pass to whichever one wants to see or eat; Perseus
steals the eye and tooth and compels them to help him in his search for Medusa.
They are grey-haired at birth, as are the babies born at the end of the Iron Race
(*WD* 181). That they are both grey-haired and "fair-cheeked" is typical of the
ambivalence which often characterizes female monsters in Greek myth; the Graeae,
the Gorgon Medusa, the viper-woman Echidna, and even the Furies can be both
beautiful and hideous.

40 The Gorgons, like the Graeae, are known for their part in the myth of Perseus,
who is sent by the king Polydectes to bring back the head of Medusa. They live
in that imaginary land far to the west (beyond the ocean) where other fantastic
and monstrous creatures dwell; Hesiod places them near (or in) the garden of the
Hesperides. Apollodorus (2.4.2) describes them as having snakes for hair, tusks like
a boar, bronze hands, and golden wings. If a Gorgon looks at someone looking at
her (i.e., if their eyes meet), that person is turned to stone.

he flew off and left the land, mother of flocks,
and came to the immortals; he lives in the house   285
of wise Zeus and carries his thunder and lightning.[41]
Chrysaor begot three-headed Geryoneus, from union
with Callirhoe, daughter of famous Ocean.
Forceful Heracles killed Geryoneus by his
rolling-gaited cattle in sea-washed Erythea   290
on the very day he drove the wide-faced cattle
to holy Tiryns, having crossed the ford of Ocean
and killed Orthus and the herdsman Eurytion
in the misty stable beyond famous Ocean.[42]
She[43] bore another unbeatable monster, in no way   295
like mortal men or immortal gods, in a
hollow cave, the divine and hard-hearted Echidna,
half a nymph with glancing eyes and lovely cheeks,
half a monstrous serpent, terrible and great, a
shimmering flesh-eater in the dark holes of holy earth.   300
There she has a cave, down under the hollow rock,
far from the immortal gods and mortal men; there
the gods allotted to her a famous house to live in.
      Grim Echidna watches in Arima under the land,
an immortal and ageless nymph for all days.   305
They say that Typhon was joined in love with her,
the arrogant and lawless monster with the glancing girl;[44]
she conceived and bore strong-hearted children:

---

41   Pegasus is best known as the winged horse on which Bellerophon rides to his heroic
      victories (Pindar, *Olympian* 13), but his usual home is the stables of Zeus.

42   Geryoneus also lives in the imaginary far west; his island Erythea (also the name of
      one of the Hesperides) is somewhere in the Atlantic. The tenth labor of Heracles is to
      capture his cattle and bring them to Eurystheus at Tiryns. To ferry the cattle from
      island to mainland, Heracles uses the golden cup of the Sun; to win the cattle he has
      to kill Geryoneus, his monstrous dog Orthus (309), and his herdsman Eurytion.

43   "She" is presumably Ceto. Echidna is another ambivalently-regarded hybrid, half-
      serpent and half-nymph. Hesiod does not specify which half is which, but the
      viper-maiden met by Heracles is described by Herodotus (4.8-10) as a woman from
      the buttocks up and a serpent below, which would conform with other composite
      monsters (Harpies, Sphinx, etc.).

44   Typhon is the greatest monster of them all, and Zeus' most formidable enemy (820-
      868). The union of Echidna and Typhon will produce four offspring who take after
      their hundred-headed father (825) in their own variable multiplicity of heads.

first she bore Orthus, the dog of Geryoneus;
next she bore the unfightable and unspeakable   310
flesh-eating Cerberus, bronze-voiced dog of Hades,
fifty-headed, shameless and strong;[45]
third she bore the ill-intended Hydra of
Lerna, whom the white-armed goddess Hera raised
in her infinite anger against forceful Heracles;   315
she died by the unfeeling bronze sword of Heracles,
son of Zeus and stepson of Amphitryon, with war-loving
Iolaus, by the designs of army-leading Athena.
She[46] bore Chimaera, who breathes furious fire,
terrible and great, swift-footed and strong,   320
with three heads, one of a hard-eyed lion,
one of a goat, one of a snake, a strong serpent;
[a lion in front, a snake behind, a goat in between,
breathing the terrible strength of blazing fire]
Pegasus and noble Bellerophon killed her.   325
And she[47] bore the deadly Sphinx, destroyer of the Cadmeians,
from union with Orthus, and the Nemean lion
whom Hera, noble wife of Zeus, raised and
settled in the hills of Nemea, a plague to men.
There he lived and ravaged the tribes of men,   330
master of Nemean Tretus and Apesas, but

---

45   Cerberus guards the entrance to the underworld, refusing to let inmates out or
      visitors in. Various sources give him from three to a hundred heads. Heracles'
      twelfth and final labor is to bring Cerberus up from the underworld.

46   The ambiguous "she" is probably Echidna, not Hydra. The word "chimaera" means
      "he-goat." Lines 323-324 are bracketed because they repeat exactly *Iliad* 6.181-182;
      they suggest that Homer, at least, believed the lion's head grew from the monster's
      neck, the goat's from its back, and the serpent's was its tail. Killing Chimaera was
      the trial imposed on Bellerophon by the Lycian king Iobates (*Iliad* 6.155-183).
      According to the Byzantine critic Tzetzes (on Lykophron 17), Bellerophon used his
      spear to lodge a piece of lead in Chimaera's throat; when her fiery breath melted the
      lead, she swallowed it and died.

47   "She" could be either Echidna or Chimaera. The Sphinx (or Phix, in Hesiod's
      Boeotian dialect) has the body of a lion, wings, and the head and breast of a
      woman. The Cadmeians are the Thebans (named after Cadmus, founder of Thebes),
      and the Sphinx is called their destroyer because she killed and ate whoever could
      not answer her famous riddle. When Oedipus finally answered correctly, she leapt
      from a height to her death (a strange sort of suicide for a winged creature).

the great strength of Heracles overcame him.[48]
    Ceto joined in love with Phorcys and bore her youngest,
a terrible serpent in the recesses of dark earth,
at the great limits, who guards the all-golden apples.[49]   335
And this is the progeny from Ceto and Phorcys.

[Birth of the Rivers]

    Tethys bore to Ocean the swirling rivers,[50]
the Nile, Alpheius, and deep-whirling Eridanus,
Strymon, Meander, and fair-flowing Ister,
Phasis, Rhesus, and silver-swirling Achelous,   340
Nessus, Rhodius, Haliacmon, Heptaporus,
Grenicus, Aesepus, and divine Simois,
Peneius, Hermus, and fair-flowing Caicus,
great Sangarius, Ladon, and Parthenius,
Euenus, Aldescus, and divine Scamander.   345
And she bore a holy race of Kourai, daughters, who on earth
raise youths to manhood, with lord Apollo
and the rivers, holding this duty from Zeus:
Persuasion (Peitho), Admete, Ianthe, and Electra,
Doris, Prymno, and Ourania of divine form,   350
Hippo, Clymene, Rhodea, and Callirhoe,
Zeuxo, Clytia, Idyia, and Pasithoe,
Plexaura, Galaxaura, and lovely Dione,
Melobosis, Thoe, and fair-figured Polydora,
Cerceis, lovely of form, and cow-eyed Pluto,   355
Perseis, Ianeira, Acaste, and Xanthe,
Petraea arousing desire, Menestho, Europa, and

---

48   The brother of the Sphinx is the Nemean lion, raised by Hera (like the Hydra) as
    a weapon in her animosity against Heracles. Heracles' first labor was to kill this
    lion, a task made more difficult by the fact that the lion's skin could not be pierced.
    Heracles therefore strangled it and from then on wore the lion-skin as his familiar
    cloak. Tretus and Apesas are mountains between Mycenae and Corinth.

49   The final child of Ceto and Phorcys is the huge serpent who guards the apples of the
    Hesperides

50   Hesiod now comes to the families of the Titans, beginning with the children of
    Ocean and Tethys. The sons are rivers and the daughters are nymphs of springs.
    Eridanus and Phasis are legendary rivers. The other 22 named rivers are divided
    between Greece, Greek Asia Minor, the Troad, Aegean Thrace and the south and
    west shores of the Black Sea. The Simois and Scamander meet each other near Troy.

Intelligence (Metis) and Eurynome, and saffron-robed Telesto,
Chryseis, Asia, and Calypso, arousing longing,
Eudora, Chance (Tuche), Amphirho, and Ocyrhoe,   360
and Styx, who is most eminent of all.[51]
These were born from Ocean and Tethys,
the eldest daughters; but there are also many others,
for Ocean has three thousand slender-ankled daughters
who, scattered over the earth and watery depths,   365
serve everywhere alike, glorious divine children.
There are as many other rivers, noisily-flowing
sons of Ocean, whom mistress Tethys bore;
it is hard for a man to say the names of them all,
but individuals know the ones by which they live.   370
Theia bore great Sun (Helius) and bright Moon (Selene)
and Dawn, who shines upon all the earth and
upon the immortal gods who hold the wide sky,
after Theia was won in love by Hyperion.
        Divine Eurybia joined in love with Crius and   375
bore Astraeus and great Pallas and Perses,
who stands out among all for his knowledge.[52]
To Astraeus Dawn bore the strong-hearted winds,
cleansing Zephyrus, the West Wind and swift-running Boreas, North Wind
and Notus, South Wind a goddess united in love with a god;   380
after these Early-born Dawn bore the star Dawn-bringer[53]
and the shining Stars the sky wears as a crown.

[The children of Styx]

Styx, daughter of Ocean, lay with Pallas and bore
Envy (Zelus) and fine-ankled Victory (Nike) in the house;
and she bore famous children, Strength and Force,   385
whose house is not apart from Zeus; they neither sit

---

51   Intelligence (Metis) will be Zeus' first wife (886), and Eurynome will be his third
     (907). Calypso is probably not the famous Calypso of *Odyssey* 5, who is usually
     called the daughter of Atlas (*Odyssey* 1.52). Styx, who is named last, is the eldest
     Oceanid (776). Why Styx is "most eminent" is explained in 389-401 and 782-806.
     Many of the Oceanids' names reflect their role as raising youths or as nymphs of
     fountains or groves.

52   The outstanding knowledge of Perses contrasts with the outstanding foolishness of
     another Perses, Hesiod's brother (*WD* 286, 397, 633).

53   Dawn-bringer (Eosphoros) is Venus, the Morning Star.

nor go, except where the god should lead them,
but always are stationed by deep-thundering Zeus.
This is what immortal Styx, daughter of Ocean, designed
on that day when the Olympian lightning-holder   390
called all the immortal gods to vast Olympus
and said whichever gods with him would fight the Titans
would not lose their honors, but each would have
the honor he held before among the immortal gods.
He said that whoever held no honor or right under Cronus   395
would enter upon honor and rights, as is just.
First immortal Styx came to Olympus
with her children, by the advice of her father;
Zeus honored her and gave outstanding gifts.
He set her to be the gods' great oath and   400
gave to her children to live with him for all days.
Just as he promised, to all without fail he
fulfilled; as for himself, he rules with great power.
     Phoebe came to Coeus' bed of much desire;
the goddess, pregnant by the god's love,   405
bore dark-robed Leto,[54] always sweet
and gentle to men and immortal gods,
sweet from the first, most mild in Olympus.
She also bore remarkable Asteria, whom Perses
led to his great house to be called his wife.   410
She conceived and bore Hecate, whom above all
Zeus, Cronus' son, honored; he gave her notable gifts,
to have a portion of the earth and barren sea.

[Hecate]

She also has a share of honor from the starry sky,
and is honored most of all by the immortal gods.[55]   415

---

54   Leto will be Zeus' sixth wife, and the mother of Apollo and Artemis (918-920).

55   The great emphasis put on the worship of Hecate and on her omnipresent power is best explained as due to Hesiod's personal interest in the goddess. The Hecate cult seems to have come to Greece from Caria in Asia Minor; if Hesiod's father was a member of the cult, this may explain why he named his other son Perses, the same name as Hecate's father. Despite the extensive praise given to Hecate, we should not suppose that Hesiod regarded her as equal to, or above, the major Olympian deities. Her status was presumably more like that of a patron saint, to whom one prays for special favors as well as for regular guidance and success in various ventures. There

For even now, whenever someone of men on earth
sacrifices fine things and prays in the way that is right,
he invokes Hecate; much honor comes to him
very easily, whose prayers the goddess favorably
receives, and she grants him wealth, since this is   420
her power. For as many were born of Earth and Sky
and obtained honor, among them all she has her due;
Cronus' son neither wronged her nor took away
what she received among the Titans, the former gods,
but this she keeps, as was the division at the beginning.   425
Nor, since she is an only child, does the goddess obtain
less honor and privileges on earth and sky and sea,
but rather she has still more, for Zeus honors her.
Greatly she assists and benefits whom she will;
she sits by revered kings in judgment, and he is   430
eminent among the people in assembly, whom she wishes;
whenever men arm for man-killing war, then
the goddess is there, and to whom she wishes
she gladly grants victory and extends glory.
She is good to stand by cavalry, by whom she wishes;   435
she is also good when men compete in the contest;
then also the goddess assists and benefits them;
one who has victory by might and strength bears off the fine
prize easily and happily, and brings glory to his parents.
To those who work the grey sea's discomfort   440
and pray to Hecate and Poseidon, the loud-sounding Earth-Shaker,
the noble goddess easily grants much catch, and
easily takes it back when it appears, if her heart wishes.
She is good, with Hermes, to increase the stock in barns;
herds of cattle and wide herds of goats and   445
flocks of wooly sheep, if her spirit wishes,
she increases from few and from many makes less.
So even though being her mother's only child, she

---

seems to be an intentional parallel between Hecate and Styx, who also received
honor and "outstanding gifts" from Zeus (399). Styx seems to have the same
function among the gods as Hecate does among mortals; each of them is invoked
on particular occasions, Styx for the oath of the gods (400) and Hecate for concrete
favors (416-421, 429-447). Hecate is also similar to Styx in that each maintains the
rights and powers she held before the reign of Zeus (Styx in 392-394).

is honored with privileges among all the immortals.
Cronus' son made her guardian of the young, who after   450
her saw with their eyes the light of much-seeing dawn.
So always she guards the young, and these are her honors.

[Birth of the Olympians; the Deception of Cronus]

Rhea, mastered by Cronus, bore illustrious children:[56]
Hestia, the Hearth,[57] Demeter,[58] and gold-sandaled Hera,[59] and

---

56   Coming now to Cronus and Rhea, Hesiod rejoins the story of the succession myth.
        We would expect the family of Cronus to come last, since he is the youngest of
        the Titans, but Hesiod puts Cronus before Iapetus so that Zeus' victory can be
        mentioned before telling the story of Iapetus' son Prometheus (a story in which
        Zeus is already king of the gods). This part of the succession myth is based largely
        on two identifiable sources, the Near Eastern myths of divine conflict and Minoan
        myths of the birth of a god in a mountain cave. For the logic of Hesiod's version,
        see the Introduction 17-18.

57   Hestia, the eldest daughter of Cronus and Rhea, has virtually no mythical function
        or role. The *Homeric Hymn to Aphrodite* mentions her, along with the other two
        famous virgin goddesses Athena and Artemis, as untouched by the "works of
        Aphrodite." Courted by both Poseidon and Apollo, she swore to Zeus that she would
        remain a virgin always; instead of marriage Zeus gave to her the right of being the
        goddess of the hearth. The hearth was the center of ritual; the city hearth, site of civic
        ritual, represented for the entire population what the private hearth in each home
        meant to the individual and family. Its fire was not allowed to go out and every day it
        was the focus (Latin *focus* = "hearth") of ritual activities such as food offerings and
        libations.

58   Demeter, the second daughter, is primarily a goddess of grain, vegetation, and
        fertility. She is best known in the myth of the loss and recovery of her daughter
        Persephone, carried off by Hades to be his bride in the underworld but ultimately
        restored to her mother. While Demeter mourns the loss of Persephone, nothing
        grows; upon their reunion the earth bursts into bloom. Demeter is a maternal
        goddess, but in a special sense: she is the mother lost by the child and the mother to
        whom one hopes to return. She will be Zeus' fourth wife (912-914).

59   Hera, Zeus' seventh and final wife (921), is primarily a goddess of weddings and
        marriage in Greek cult. In myth she is the powerful wife of Zeus, but both her
        power and her status as wife are more negative than positive. She is rarely maternal
        (see on 922), but is usually a hostile and resentful stepmother. Her anger is aimed
        chiefly at Zeus' many illegitimate children, whose rise to heroic status is in large
        part the result of their attempts to resist, avoid, or placate her fury.

strong Hades,[60] who lives in a palace under the land   455
and has a pitiless heart, and Poseidon, loud-sounding Earth-Shaker[61]
and wise Zeus,[62] the father of gods and men,
by whose thunder the wide lands are shaken.
Great Cronus would swallow these, as each
would come from the holy womb to his mother's knees,   460
intending this, that none of Sky's proud line but
himself would hold the honor of king over the immortals.[63]
For he learned from Earth and starry Sky
that it was fate that his own son would master him,
although he was powerful, by the counselling of great Zeus.   465
So he kept no blind man's watch, but alertly
swallowed his own children; incurable grief held Rhea.
But when she was about to bear Zeus, father of gods
and men, she begged her own dear parents,
Earth and starry Sky, to help her think   470
of some wisdom, by which she might secretly have
her son, and make great crooked-minded Cronus pay the
Furies of her father and the children he swallowed.[64]

60   Hades is the god of death and the underworld; his name seems to mean the
      "Unseen One" and the Greeks were generally reluctant to call him by name,
      preferring instead to use euphemisms like "Master of Many," "Receiver of
      Many," and the "Rich One". He appears rarely in myth, since he rarely leaves his
      underworld palace; the one notable exception is his brief appearance on earth to
      carry off Demeter's daughter Persephone.

61   Poseidon, the "Earth-Shaker," is the chief among several gods of the sea; we have
      already seen Sea (Pontus), Ocean (Oceanus), and Nereus, and there are others.
      Poseidon is also associated with earthquakes and with horses. In general Poseidon,
      like the storm-god Zeus, is a god of force; he is the god who brings sea-storms and
      earthquakes (or averts their harm), and in his sexual encounters he overcomes
      monsters such as Medusa or takes the form of a stallion.

62   Zeus is a sky-god like his grandfather Sky (Ouranos), associated especially with
      rain, storms, and lightning. He is king of the gods because he is most powerful, but
      he is also most wise. He seems to be connected with no particular city or region,
      but is the most panhellenic of the gods.

63   For Cronus' strategy see the Introduction, p. 18-19. There are similarities between
      the story of Cronus swallowing his children and the Hurrian myth of Kumarbi and
      the children who grew inside him.

64   The Furies are the spirits of guilt and retribution whose presence is the result
      of Cronus' misdeeds against his father and his children (see on 178-187). The
      "wisdom" (metis) discovered here will later become Zeus' wife and then be
      swallowed by him (*Th* 886-99).

They heard and obeyed their dear daughter
and told her what was destined to happen   475
concerning king Cronus and his strong-hearted son.
They sent her to Lyctus, to the rich land of Crete,
when she was about to bear her youngest son,
great Zeus; vast Earth received him from her
in wide Crete to tend and raise.   480
Carrying him through the swift black night, she came
first to Lyctus; taking him in her arms, she hid him
in a deep cave, down in dark holes of holy earth,
on Mount Aegean, dense with woods.
Rhea wrapped a huge stone in a baby's robe, and fed it   485
to Sky's wide-ruling son, lord of the earlier gods;
he took it in his hands and put it down his belly,
the fool; he did not think in his mind that instead
of a stone his own son, undefeated and secure, was left
behind, soon to master him by force and violence and   490
drive him from his honor, and be lord of the immortals himself.
        Swiftly then the strength and noble limbs
of the future lord grew; at the end of a year,
tricked by the clever advice of Earth,
great crooked-minded Cronus threw up his children,   495
defeated by the craft and force of his own son.
First he vomited out the stone he had swallowed last;
Zeus fixed it firmly in the wide-pathed land
at sacred Pytho in the vales of Parnassus,
to be a sign thereafter, a wonder to mortal men.[65]   500
        He released from their deadly chains his uncles,[66]
Sky's sons, whom their father mindlessly bound.
They did not forget gratitude for his help,
and gave him thunder and the fiery lightning-bolt

---

[65] The stone disgorged by Cronus was exhibited at Delphi, where Pausanias saw it
      (10.24). Parnassus is the mountain of Delphi, and Pytho, at first the general area
      around Delphi, became an alternate name for Delphi itself. There was a more famous
      stone at Delphi, the *omphalos* (navel-stone) which marked Delphi as the center of the
      earth. Pausanias (10.16) distinguishes the *omphalos* from the stone of Cronus, but
      Pausanias is almost 900 years later than Hesiod, who perhaps identifies the two.

[66] The "uncles" (501) must be the Cyclopes, who were imprisoned in Tartarus by Sky
      and who will give Zeus the lightning (504-505); the freeing of their brothers, the
      Hundred-Handed, will be reported in 617-626.

and lightning, which vast Earth earlier had hidden;   505
trusting in these, he is lord of mortals and immortals.

[The Children of Iapetus]

Iapetus married the fine-ankled daughter of Ocean,
Clymene, and went up to the same bed;
she bore him a son, strong-hearted Atlas, and
she bore all-eminent Menoetius, and Prometheus, Forethought,   510
subtle and devious, and wrong-thinking Epimetheus, Afterthought,
who was from the first an evil for men who work for food;[67]
he first received from Zeus the molded woman,
the maiden. Wide-seeing Zeus sent arrogant Menoetius
down to Erebus, striking him with a smoking thunderbolt,   515
for his recklessness and excessive pride.
And Atlas, standing at the limits of the earth,
before the clear-voiced Hesperides, under strong necessity,
holds the wide sky with head and untiring arms;
for this is the fate wise Zeus allotted him.   520

[Prometheus, the Origin of Sacrifice, Fire and the First Woman]

He bound devious Prometheus with inescapable
harsh bonds, fastened through the middle of a column,
and he inflicted on him a long-winged eagle, which ate
his immortal liver; but it grew as much in all
at night as the long-winged bird would eat all day.[68]   525

---

67   After hinting at Zeus' inevitable victory (506), Hesiod interrupts the story of
      conflict between Zeus and his father to introduce the conflict between Zeus and
      Prometheus. First, however, he must finish the account of the genealogy of the
      Titans; Iapetus, the one remaining Titan son, will be the father of Prometheus.
      Clymene is the Oceanid of 351. In the *Odyssey* (1.52-54) Atlas is the father of
      Calypso and holds up the pillars which separate earth and sky. In 746-748
      Atlas will be situated somewhere in the underworld, but here he is placed with
      the Hesperides in their garden in the far west. The sky-holding is evidently a
      punishment, since Atlas is "under strong compulsion," but the reason for his
      punishment is even less clear than in the case of Menoetius.

68   Although the scene of Prometheus' punishment is said in almost all accounts to
      be the Caucasus Mountains (or Scythia, which may be the same), there seems to
      be another version in which he, like Atlas, is at the western ends of the earth. This
      is the site of the garden of the Hesperides, and it is during Heracles' search for this
      garden that he encounters Prometheus. The most famous version of Prometheus'
      punishment, Aeschylus' *Prometheus Bound*, is set in Scythia.

Heracles, the mighty son of fine-ankled Alcmene,
killed it and freed from his evil sickness the son
of Iapetus and released him from anguish
by the will of high-ruling Olympian Zeus,
so that the glory of Theban-born Heracles   530
would be more than before on the nurturing land;[69]
thinking of this, he honored his famous son, and
though he was angry quit the rage he had ever since
the Titan contended in counsel with Cronus' mighty son.
For when gods and mortal men made a settlement   535
at Mecone, then he cleverly cut up a big ox and
set it before them, trying to deceive the mind of Zeus.[70]
For Zeus he set out meat and innards rich with fat
on the skin, covering it with the stomach of the ox;
but for men he set the white ox-bones, with deceitful craft   540
arranging them well and covering them with shining fat.
Then the father of men and gods said to him:
        "Son of Iapetus, distinguished of all lords,
sir, how unfairly you divided the portions."   544
        Thus Zeus, knowing deathless plans, spoke and mocked him.
But crooked-minded Prometheus answered him, gently
smiling, and did not forget his deceitful craft:
        "Zeus, most famed and greatest of eternal gods,
take of these whichever the spirit within tells you."
        He spoke with the trick in mind; but Zeus, knowing deathless   550
plans, knew and did not miss the trick; in his heart
he foresaw evils which were going to happen to mortal men.[71]

---

69   Heracles, the greatest hero of Greek myth, is the son of Zeus and Alcmene. He is
      usually said to have released Prometheus during his eleventh labor (the golden
      apples of the Hesperides). Although there may seem to be a contradiction between
      this account of Heracles' killing the eagle and freeing Prometheus "from evil
      suffering" and the later statement that "great bondage holds" Prometheus (616),
      the present tense "holds" seems to be a moralizing coda finishing the story with a
      general principle.

70   The meeting between men and gods at Mecone marks the end of the time when
      men and gods lived and ate together; the period before their separation may be the
      time of Hesiod's Golden Race (WD 109-126). Mecone is the old name for Sicyon, a
      city near Corinth in the northeast Peloponnesus.

71   Hesiod's version may be an attempt to rescue Zeus, the hero of his poem, from the
      appearance of being duped.

With both hands he lifted up the white fat,
but he was angry in mind and rage came to his spirit,
when he saw the white ox-bones of the deceitful craft.   555
Therefore the tribes of men on the land burn to the
immortals white bones on reeking altars.
Greatly angry, cloud-gatherer Zeus said to him:
      "Son of Iapetus, knowing thoughts beyond all,
sir, you still have not forgotten your craft and deceit."   560
      So spoke angry Zeus, who knows deathless plans;
from then on, never forgetting the trick, he would
not give the strength of untiring fire to ash-trees
for mortal men, who live on the land.[72]
But the great son of Iapetus deceived him   565
and stole the far-seen light of untiring fire
in a hollow narthex;[73] this bit deep in the spirit
of high-thundering Zeus and his heart was angry
when he saw the far-seen light of fire among men.
In return for fire, he quickly made an evil for men;   570
for Hephaestus, the famous Lame One made from earth the likeness
of a revered modest maiden, by the counsels of Cronus' son.

---

72   It is unclear whether men had fire before and Zeus now deprives them of it, or if
      they had never possessed it. The reference to "ash-trees" (563) may refer to a belief
      that originally fire was present within trees; such a belief no doubt goes back to a
      time when fire was procured from lightning-struck trees. Myths of the theft of fire
      are found among primitive cultures on every inhabited continent. Sometimes the
      thief is a culture-hero like Prometheus, but typically it is an animal, most often a
      bird or insect (because of their ability to fly from earth to sky and back). Because of
      the necessity of fire for many of the technical advances of civilization, the thief of
      fire may become a culture-hero like Prometheus, who is said by Aeschylus to have
      taught men woodworking, astronomy, mathematics, the domestication of animals,
      navigation, medicine, prophecy, and metallurgy, in addition to giving them fire and
      "blind hopes" (*Prometheus Bound* 436-506).

73   A narthex is the giant fennel plant; its slowly combustible interior and hard rind
      make it an appropriate vessel in which to carry and conceal fire.

Bright-eyed Athena sashed her and dressed her[74]
in silver clothes; she placed with her hands a
decorated veil on her head, marvelous to see;   575
[and fresh garlands of longing, the flowers of plants,
Pallas Athena put around her head][75]
and she placed on her head a golden crown
which Hephaestus, the famous Lame One, had made himself,
shaping it with his hands, doing grace to father Zeus.   580
On it he carved many designs, a marvelous sight;
of all dread beasts the land and sea nourish,
he included most, amazingly similar to living
animals with voices; and grace breathed over all.
    But when he made the lovely evil to pay for the good,   585
he led her where the other gods and men were;[76]
she delighted in the finery from the great father's
bright-eyed daughter; awe filled immortal gods and mortal
men when they saw the sheer trick, irresistible to men.
For from her is the race of female women,   590
[from her is the deadly race and tribes of women][77]
a great plague to mortals, dwelling with men,
not suited for cursed poverty, but for wealth.
As when bees in covered hives feed

---

74   This line reappears as *WD* 72. Athena and Hephaestus, the two gods most closely
      associated with crafts, are entrusted with the creation, dressing, and adornment of
      Pandora. In *WD* 60-82 a divine task force joins in this work, including Hephaestus
      (60), Athena (63), Aphrodite (65), Hermes (67), the Graces and Persuasion (73),
      and the Seasons (75). In addition to an elaborate adornment scene, the *WD* version
      adds other details: the name Pandora is given to the woman (who is unnamed in
      the *Theogony*) because all the gods "presented a gift" (82); Pandora is received by
      Epimetheus, and opens a jar, allowing all evils and diseases to escape, but retaining
      Hope within the jar (94-104).

75   These lines are suspected by most editors because of the repetition of Athena's
      name in 573 and 577.

76   If before Pandora mankind lived in a Golden Age (see *WD* 90-2), this would explain
      why men and gods are together when Pandora is brought out for exhibition.

77   The *Theogony* version is much more misogynistic that the *WD* version. In the
      latter the evils come from the jar which Pandora unfortunately opens, but here it
      is woman herself who is a great evil to man. This evil, it turns out, is the old-age
      complaint (of envious men) that women are idle consumers of the wealth a man has
      worked hard to amass. Since 590 and 591 are alternate expressions, one of the lines
      is presumably not genuine.

the drones, companions of evil works, 595
the bees work until sunset, all day
and every day, and make the pale combs,
while the drones stay inside, in the covered hives,
harvesting the work of others into their own stomachs;
similarly for mortal men, high-thundering Zeus 600
made an evil: women, the partners of distressing works.
He gave a second evil to balance a good,[78]
since whoever escapes marriage and women's harm,
by refusing to marry, comes to deadly old age
with no son to tend him; not lacking livelihood 605
while he lives, when he dies distant kin divide
his estate. But even the man whose fate is to marry
and acquires a good wife, suited to his wants,
for him from the first good and evil are balanced
always; but whoever acquires the wicked kind 610
lives with unending trouble in his mind and
spirit and heart, and the evil is incurable.
So it is impossible to steal away or surpass the mind of Zeus.
For not even Iapetus' son, good Prometheus,
escaped his heavy anger, but of necessity 615
great bondage holds him, though he knows many things.

[Zeus Frees the Hundred-Handed Ones]

When first the father was angry at heart with Briareus
and Cottus and Gyges, he bound them in strong bondage;
when he noticed their great manhood, their looks
and size, he put them under the wide-pathed land.[79] 620

---

78   The "second evil" (602) is lack of a son (605), and the "good" (602) is managing
to escape marriage and to live alone. If someone avoids the first evil (woman) by
remaining single, he will receive the second evil from Zeus, the absence of a son to
take care of him in his old age and maintain his estate after he has died.

79   The digression on Prometheus and the creation of woman has completed the
genealogies of the Titans, and Hesiod returns to the war between the Olympians
and the Titans (the Titanomachy), which was about to begin at 506. Myths world-
wide contain stories of a war between the gods at the beginning (or end) of the
world. Having already released the Cyclopes and acquired a lightning supply (501-
506), Zeus releases the three Hundred-Handed, who will be his heavy artillery.
The Hundred-Handed will play a large role in the war (only they and Zeus are
mentioned as fighting on the Olympian side), while the Cyclopes disappear from
view, their lightning now in the hands of Zeus.

They lived there under the land in pain,
at the farthest borders of the great earth,
suffering much and long, with great grief of heart.
But Cronus' son and the other immortal gods,
whom fair-haired Rhea bore in Cronus' love,   625
brought them up to the light, by Earth's counsel.
For she told them everything in detail, how with
their help they would win victory and bright fame.
For a long time they fought in bitter toil
against one another in strong battles,   630
the Titan gods and those born of Cronus,
the proud Titans from lofty Othrys
and from Olympus the gods, givers of good,
whom fair-haired Rhea bore, having lain with Cronus.
With bitter war against one another   635
they fought continually for ten full years;[80]
there was no end or relief from harsh strife
for either, the war's outcome was evenly balanced.
But when he gave them everything fitting,
nectar and ambrosia, which the gods eat themselves,   640
and the proud spirit grew in the breasts of all,
[when they tasted nectar and lovely ambrosia]
then the father of gods and men said to them:
        "Hear me, good children of Earth and Sky,
that I may say what the spirit in my chest commands.   645
For a long time now against one another
we have fought every day for victory and power,
the Titan gods and we born of Cronus.
Show your great force and unbeatable arms
against the Titans in savage war;   650
remember our friendship, and how much you suffered
before you came to the light from grievous bondage
under the murky gloom, thanks to our counsels."
        When he had spoken, blameless Cottus replied:
        "Divine one, you tell us what we know; on our own   655
we know your superior mind and thoughts, and
that you defended the immortals from icy harm;

---

80   We learn now that the war has already lasted for ten years when Zeus learns from
      Earth of the need for the Hundred-Handed. The Trojan War also lasts for ten years.

by your counsels we came back from the murky gloom,
back from the unyielding bonds, obtaining
the unexpected, lord son of Cronus.   660
So now with firm mind and willing spirit
we will defend your power in hostile war,
fighting the Titans in strong battles."

[The War with the Titans]

After he spoke, the gods who give good welcomed
the speech they heard; their spirit longed for war   665
even more than before, and they roused grim fighting
that same day, all of them, female as well as male,
the Titan gods against those born of Cronus and
those Zeus brought to light from darkness
under the land, dread and strong, with huge strength.   670
A hundred arms shot from the shoulders
of each and all, fifty heads grew from the
shoulders of each, from their massive bodies.
They stood against the Titans in grim battle,
holding great rocks in their massive hands;   675
the Titans opposite brought force to their ranks
expectantly; both displayed the deeds of arms
and strength together, and the vast sea echoed loudly
and the earth resounded greatly, and the wide sky
shook and groaned, and great Olympus was shaken   680
from its foundation by the immortals' charge; a heavy
tremor of feet reached dim Tartarus, and the loud
noise of unspeakable rout and strong weapons.
So they hurled at each other the painful weapons;
shouts from both sides reached starry Sky,   685
as they came together with a great outcry.
Zeus no longer restrained his might, but now his
heart was filled with wrath, and he revealed all
his force; from the sky and Olympus both,
he came throwing a lightning-flurry; the bolts   690
flew thick with thunder and lightning
from his massive hand, whirling a holy flame,
one after another; the life-giving earth resounded
in flames, the vast woods crackled loudly about,
all the land and Ocean's streams and the   695

barren sea were boiling; the hot blast enveloped
the land-born Titans, the flame reached the upper
brightness in its fury; although they were strong, the blazing
glow of thunder and lightning blinded their eyes.
The awful heat seized Chasm;[81] it seemed,   700
for eyes to see and ears to hear the sound,
just as if earth and wide sky from above came
together; for so great a noise would arise
from the one fallen upon and the other falling down;
such a noise arose from the strife of clashing gods.   705
The winds stirred up earthquake and dust and
thunder and lighting and blazing lightning-bolt,
the weapons of great Zeus, and brought the shout
and cry into the midst of both sides; a great din
arose from fearful strife, and strength's work was revealed.   710
        But the tide of the fighting was turned; before, in mutual
collision, they fought continuously in strong battles;
but now in the front ranks they roused dread war,
Cottus and Briareus and Gyges, hungry for war.[82]
They threw three hundred rocks from massive hands   715
at once, and with their missiles overshadowed
the Titans; they sent them under the wide-pathed
land, and bound them in cruel bonds,
having defeated them by force, despite their daring,
as far below the earth as sky is above the earth;[83]   720
for it is that far from the earth to dim Tartarus.

---

81   Chasm (Chaos) is mentioned not because we are expected to know the exact
     location of the first being, but to indicate the enormous space which felt the blast of
     heat. Chasm is somewhere in the underworld (814), and presumably far below the
     surface of the earth; the heat extends even down to Chasm, just as it reaches up to
     the "upper air" [aether, 697].

82   Now that Zeus seems to have won the war, the Hundred-Handed are re-introduced
     to finish the job and to fulfill Earth's prophecy (626-628).

83   We should assume, I think, that the underworld is everything below the earth's
     surface, that Tartarus is Hesiod's name for the underworld, that the Titans are
     put in a prison at the farthest point of Tartarus, that Hades, Night, Styx, etc.,
     are outside the prison but inside Tartarus, that the roots, or sources, of the four
     cosmological divisions are in Tartarus (that is, they all reach beneath the earth's
     surface), that even Chasm is located in Tartarus. In later Greek thought, the prison
     itself is called Tartarus and receives new inhabitants, and the entire underworld
     comes to be called Hades.

[Tartarus]

A bronze anvil falling for nine nights and days
from the sky would reach the earth on the tenth;[84]
and a bronze anvil falling for nine nights and days
from the earth would reach Tartarus on the tenth. 725
Around it runs a bronze fence; and about its
neck flows night in a triple row; while above
grow the roots of earth and the barren sea.
    There the Titan gods under the dim gloom
are hid away by the counsels of cloud-gatherer Zeus, 730
in a moldy place, the limits of vast earth.
For them is no escape, since Poseidon put in
bronze doors, and the fence runs on both sides.
    [There Gyges, Cottus, and great-spirited Briareus
live, the faithful guards of aegis-bearing Zeus.][85] 735
    There dark earth and dim Tartarus
and the barren sea and starry sky
all have their sources and limits in a row,
terrible and dank, which even the gods abhor;
[the gap is great, and not until a year's end 740
would a man reach the bottom, if first he were within
the doors, but terrible gust after gust would carry him
here and there; it is awful even for the immortal gods]
[this is monstrous; and the terrible house
of dim Night stands covered in dark clouds] 745
    In front Atlas, the son of Iapetus, holds the wide sky
with his head and untiring arms, standing
immobile, where Night and Day come near and

---

84   The number ten seems to be a popular choice for mythic expressions of great
      magnitude or duration. The anvil falls for nine days and lands on the tenth, the
      Titan-War and Trojan War last for ten years apiece, and the prophet Teiresias,
      asked whether men or women get greater pleasure in sex, answers that on a scale
      of ten men are one and women are nine (Apollodorus 3.6.7). Any discussion of the
      significance of the number ten and the ratio 9:1 should bear in mind that by the
      Greek method of reckoning time a child is born in the tenth month of its mother's
      pregnancy (e.g., the *Homeric Hymn to Hermes* 11 where Hermes is born in the
      "tenth moon").

85   These lines are bracketed because they seem contradicted at 815-819, but the two
      passages may express the same notion in different forms.

address one another, passing the great threshold
of bronze; one will go down in, the other comes from   750
the door, and the house never holds both within,
but always one is out of the house and
traverses the land, while the other is in the house
and awaits the time in season of her journey, when it will come;
one holds much-seeing light for those on earth,   755
the other, who holds in her arms Sleep, brother of
Death, is deadly Night, covered in misty cloud.
     There the children of dark Night have their homes,
Sleep and Death, awful gods; never does
shining Sun look on them with his beams,   760
as he goes up to the sky or comes down from the sky.
The former crosses the earth and wide backs of
the sea harmless and gentle to men, but the
other's heart is iron, and his bronze heart is
pitiless in his chest; he holds whomever he once   765
seizes of men; he is hateful even to the immortal gods.
     There in front the echoing homes of the god under the land
[of mighty Hades and awesome Persephone]
stand, and a terrible dog is on guard in front,
unpitying possessor of an evil trick; on those   770
going in he fawns with his tail and both ears, but
does not let them go back out and, waiting,
eats whomever he catches going out the doors.
[of mighty Hades and awesome Persephone]
     There dwells a goddess hated by the immortals,   775
terrible Styx, eldest daughter of back-flowing
Ocean;[86] away from the gods she lives in a noble
house, roofed with great rocks; on all sides
it reaches up to the sky with silver pillars.
Rarely does Iris, swift-footed daughter of Thaumas,   780
come as messenger over the sea's wide backs.
Whenever quarrels and strife arise among the immortals
and one of those who have Olympian homes should lie,

---

86   Ocean is called "back-flowing" because he circles the earth and flows back into
       himself. For Iris as messenger, see n38. That Iris must travel across the sea to reach
       Styx suggests again that the underworld (or its entrance) is located, at least in part,
       at the farthest limits of the earth's surface.

Zeus sends Iris to bring the gods' great oath
from afar in a golden pitcher, the famous cold   785
water which trickles down from a high steep
rock; far below the wide-pathed land it
flows from the holy river through black night;
a branch of Ocean, a tenth portion is allotted to it;
nine parts winding around the earth and sea's wide   790
backs in silver eddies fall into the sea, but the
tenth flows out from the rock, a great woe to the gods.[87]
Whoever pours libation and breaks his oath, of the
immortals who hold the peaks of snowy Olympus,
lies unbreathing until the year's end;   795
he never comes near ambrosia and nectar
for food, but lies unbreathing and unspeaking
on a covered bed, and an evil coma covers him.
But when he ends being sick for a great year,
another harsher ordeal succeeds the first;   800
for nine years he is parted from the gods who always
are, and never joins in council and feasts,
for nine full years; in the tenth he rejoins the
meetings of the immortals who have Olympian homes.
The gods made the eternal and primal water of Styx   805
such an oath; it emerges through a forbidding place.[88]

      There dark earth and dim Tartarus
and the barren sea and starry sky
all have their sources and limits in a row,
terrible and dank, which even the gods abhor.   810
There are shining gates and a bronze threshold
with never-ending roots, unmoveable and
natural; beyond and far from all the gods
live the Titans, past gloomy Chasm.
But the famous helpers of loud-thundering Zeus   815
live in houses on Ocean's foundations,

---

87   Styx was appointed the gods' oath at 400. By pouring a libation consisting of the
      water of Styx (793), a god commits himself to the punishment described in 795-803
      if he should swear falsely.

88   The water of Styx is immortal because the goddess Styx is immortal. In much later
      myths the immortality of this water could be transferred to someone (e.g., Achilles)
      who was dipped in it.

Cottus and Gyges; but Poseidon, the deep-roaring Earth-Shaker
made Briareus his son-in-law for his courage,
and gave him his daughter Cymopolea to marry.

[Typhon's Challenge to Zeus]

But when Zeus drove the Titans from the sky,   820
vast Earth bore her youngest child Typhon
from the love of Tartarus, through golden Aphrodite;[89]
his hands are strong, to do his work, and the
strong god's legs never tire; from his shoulders
grew a hundred snake-heads, a dread serpent's   825
with dark and lambent tongues; his eyes
under the brows on the awesome heads shot fire;
[from all the heads fire blazed as he glowered]
from all the dread heads came voices which
spoke all unspeakable sounds; at one time,   830
they made sounds the gods understand; at another,
the sound of a proud bellowing bull, unstoppable
in wrath; at another, a lion with shameless spirit;
again, sounds like a pack of dogs, marvelous to hear;
again, he would hiss and high mountains re-echoed.   835
A deed past help would have happened that day
and he would have been lord over immortals and mortals,
if the father of men and gods had not thought quickly.
He thundered hard and strong, and all the earth
resounded horribly, and the wide sky above and   840
sea and Ocean's streams and earth's lowest parts.
Great Olympus trembled under the immortal feet
of the lord setting out, and the land groaned.
Heat from both of them seized the violent sea,
from thunder and lightning, from the monster's fire,   845

---

89   Zeus must now fight one last battle before he can settle down to the business of
ruling and procreating. Angered by the defeat of the Titans, Earth mates with
Tartarus and produces Typhon, the most formidable monster of them all. In
later accounts, the war between Zeus and Typhon is more complicated and of
less certain outcome than in Hesiod's version; for Hesiod, however, the battle is
decided as soon as Zeus exerts his full power (853-855), just as he had won the
Titanomachy by throwing off restraint and attacking in full force (687-689). The
Typhon-War, in fact, is very much a repetition of the Titan-War, and Typhon will
end up in Tartarus with the Titans

from searing winds and from the fiery lightning-bolt.
The whole earth was boiling, and the sky and sea;
great waves raged around and over the coasts from
the immortals' attack, and endless rumbling arose;
Hades, lord of the dead below, trembled, and so   850
did the Titans around Cronus in Tartarus,
from the endless noise and awful war.
        When the anger of Zeus reached its height,
he seized his weapons, thunder and lighting and
lightning-bolt, leaped from Olympus, and struck;   855
he burned all the dread monster's unspeakable heads.
When he had whipped him and mastered him with blows,
he threw him down crippled, and great Earth groaned.
Fire poured from the thunderstruck lord
in the dark rugged glens of the mountain where   860
he was hit, and the vast earth burned widely
from unspeakable heat, and melted as tin
is melted in well-bored crucibles by workmen's
craft, or as iron, strongest of all things,
is mastered by burning fire in mountain glens   865
in the holy land, by the arts of Hephaestus;
so the earth melted in the glare of blazing fire.
And Zeus, vexed in spirit, threw him into wide Tartarus.
        From Typhon is the strength of wet-blowing winds,
except Notus, the south wind, and Boreas from the north,
and Zephyrus, the clearing west wind;   870
these are a kind from the gods, a great help to mortals.[90]
But the other winds blow false on the sea;
some fall upon the misty sea, a great plague
to mortals, and they rage with evil storm;
they blow unpredictably, scattering ships and   875
killing sailors; there is no defense against
their evil for men who meet them on the sea.
And other winds on the vast flowering earth
destroy the beautiful fields of earth-born men,
filling them with dust and terrible tumult.   880
        But when the blessed gods had finished their toil

---

90   The good winds Notus, Boreas, and Zephyrus are the sons of Astraeus and Dawn
        (378-380).

and decided the matter of honors with the Titans
by force, they urged wide-seeing Olympian Zeus
to be king and lord of the immortals, by Earth's
advice; and he divided their honors among them.[91]   885

[Zeus' Wives and Children]

Zeus, king of gods, made Metis, Intelligence, his first wife,
she who knows most of gods and mortal men.
But when she was about to bear the bright-eyed
goddess Athena, then he deceived her mind with a
trick of wily words, and put her down in his belly,   890
by the advice of Earth and starry Sky. Thus
they advised him, so that no other of the eternal
gods would hold the kingly honor but Zeus.[92]
For from her wise children were fated to be born:
first a daughter, bright-eyed Tritogeneia, Athena,[93]   895
like her father in strength and wise counsel,
but then she was going to bear a son
proud of heart, king of gods and men;

---

91   Hesiod's brief reference to Zeus' division of the gods' honors is expressed more
      specifically and somewhat differently in *Iliad* 15.187-193, where Poseidon describes
      the division of the world by lot between himself and his two brothers.

92   Having succeeded to the position of king of the gods, Zeus is still not entirely
      secure. His father and grandfather also ruled, but were deposed by their sons.
      Zeus needs both strength and strategic knowledge to protect his kingship; his
      power was evident in the wars with the Titans and Typhon, and his acquisition of
      knowledge is now demonstrated, at least symbolically, in the outcome of his first
      marriage. Intelligence (Metis) has two important functions: she is destined to
      bear a son who will replace Zeus as king of gods and men (897-898), and she, who
      "knows most" (887), is the personification of practical wisdom (*metis*), the art of
      knowing what to do with what one learns. Zeus exhibits his *metis* both practically
      and metaphorically: first, by following the advice of Earth and thereby preventing
      the birth of the ominous son, and second, by swallowing Intelligence and thus
      incorporating within himself the *metis* she represents. The child Intelligence is
      pregnant with when Zeus swallows her is Athena, whose birth from Zeus' head will
      be recounted in 924-926.

93   Athena's epithet "Tritogeneia" may mean "born by the river Triton," but this is by
      no means certain.

but first Zeus put her into his own belly,
so the goddess might advise him on good and evil.[94]   900

• • • • •

　　Second, he married sleek Right, who bore the Seasons,
Good-governance and Justice and blooming Peace,
who tend the works of mortal men, and the
Fates, to whom wise Zeus gave most honor,   904
Clotho the Spinner and Lachesis the Alotter and Atropos the Unbending,
who give mortal men to have both good and evil.[95]
　　Eurynome, Ocean's daughter of fairest form,
bore to him the three fair-cheeked Graces,
Splendor and Gladness, and lovely Thalia, Festivity;
limb-loosening eros poured from their glancing   910
eyes; beautifully they glanced under their brows.[96]
　　Next he came to the bed of nurturant Demeter;
she bore white-armed Persephone, whom Hades, Aidoneus
seized from her mother; but wise Zeus allowed it.[97]

94　For a variety of reasons, it is generally agreed that the ending of the *Theogony*
　　was not written by Hesiod, but there is general disagreement as to where what
　　remains of the original *Theogony* ends and the later revision begins. In addition
　　to the original ending of the *Theogony*, now lost, Hesiod may also have composed
　　something like the *Catalogue of Women*, fragments of which survive, as introduced
　　by the last lines of the *Theogony*.

95　Right (Themis), Zeus' second wife, is of the Titan generation (135). As in the
　　case of Intelligence, her name indicates the benefit Zeus derives from alliance
　　with her; *themis* means "right" or "established custom." The Seasons are in cult
　　principally goddesses of the vegetative cycle (their Athenian cult names Thallo
　　and Carpo mean "flourish" and "bear fruit"). The names given to them in the
　　Theogony suggest that they function in civic and political life as well, another area
　　in which regularity and predictability are essential. The Fates (Moirae) were earlier
　　called daughters of Night (217); the inconsistency may be due to negligence or to
　　the poet's wish to present an alternate version. As their names suggest, they are
　　the determiners of a lifetime, visualized as a thread which one spins, the second
　　measures, and the third fixes at the measured length, often by cutting it

96　The third wife is the Oceanid Eurynome, whose three daughters are the Graces
　　— Aglaea (Splendor), Euphrosyne (Gladness), Thalia (Festivity or Good-cheer),
　　personifications of everything that is beautiful and graceful in nature and human
　　life. The description in 910-911 emphasizes their erotic attractiveness and
　　desirability, and they appear often as attendants of Aphrodite.

97　Zeus' fourth wife is his sister Demeter. The abduction of their daughter Persephone
　　by Hades, with the connivance of Zeus, is narrated most fully in the *Homeric
　　Hymn to Demeter*. Aidoneus is a lengthened form of the name Hades.

Then he loved fair-haired Memory, who bore   915
the nine Muses with golden headbands,
whose delight is banquets and the pleasure of song.[98]
    And Leto, joined in love to aegis-bearing Zeus,
bore Apollo and archeress Artemis, arousing longing,
children beyond all of Sky's descendants.   920
    Lastly he made Hera his blooming wife;
she bore goddess Youth (Hebe) and Ares, the war god
and Eileithyia, the Goddess of Childbirth
having joined in love with the king of gods and men.
    He himself bore from his head bright-eyed Athena,
the awesome, fight-rousing, army-leading, unweary   925
mistress whose delight is din and wars and fighting;
but Hera, who was angry and at odds with her husband,
without love's union bore famous Hephaestus,
excellent in craft beyond all of Sky's descendants.[99]
    From Amphitrite and Poseidon, loud-sounding Earth-Shaker   930
was born great and mighty Triton, who in the sea's
depth lives with his mother and lord father in
golden homes, an awful god.[100] But to Ares, piercer
of shields, Aphrodite of Cythera bore Fear and Terror,
terrible ones who rout the dense ranks of men in   935
cold war with city-destroying Ares, and she bore
Harmonia, whom high-spirited Cadmus took as his wife.
    And the child of Atlas, Maia, bore to Zeus glorious Hermes,
herald of the gods, after going up to his holy bed.
    And the child of Cadmus, Semele, bore an illustrious son, much-   940
cheering Dionysus, after joining Zeus in love,

---

98   For Memory (Mnemosyne) and the Muses, see above, notes 14, 15.

99   Since Athena has apparently been inside Zeus during six marriages, it is perhaps
      not surprising that artistic and literary representations of her birth portray her as
      a fully-grown, fully-armed adult. Either Hephaestus (Pindar, *Olympian* 7.65) or
      Prometheus (Euripides, *Ion* 454) splits open Zeus' head with an axe, so that Athena
      can be born. Hera's quarrel with Zeus is the result of his having given birth to
      Athena; since he seems no longer to need a woman to produce a child, she decides
      to show him that she does not need a man to bear a child herself.

100   Finished with the children of Zeus and Hera, Hesiod moves to Zeus' brother
      Poseidon (Earth-Shaker); Hades and Persephone have no children, the only
      instance in Greek myth of a fruitless divine union. Amphitrite is a Nereid (243).

mortal with immortal; now they both are gods.[101]

And Alcmene bore forceful Heracles, having
joined in love with cloud-gathering Zeus.

[Children of the Gods]

And Hephaestus, the famous lame god, made Aglaea,   945
youngest of the Graces, his blooming wife.

And gold-haired Dionysus took auburn Ariadne,
daughter of Minos, as his blooming wife;
Cronus' son made her immortal and ageless for him.[102]

The strong son of fair-ankled Alcmene, mighty   950
Heracles, having finished his painful ordeals, took
Youth, child of great Zeus and gold-sandaled Hera,
as his modest wife in snowy Olympus; he is
happy, who finished his great work and lives with
the immortals, carefree and ageless for all days.[103]   955

To untiring Sun the famed child of Ocean, Perseis
bore Circe and the king Aeetes.
Aeetes, son of Sun who shines on mortals,
by the gods' counsels married fair-cheeked Idyia,
the daughter of the perfect river Ocean;   960

---

101   Semele is the daughter of Cadmus and Harmonia; from the ashes of the thunder-
      struck Semele, Zeus rescued the fetus, put it in his thigh, and later gave birth to the
      god Dionysus (Euripides, *Bacchae* 88-100). The deification of Semele seems to be
      due to the fact that she was consumed by Zeus' lightning (Pindar, *Olympian* 2.25),
      rather than to her role as mother of Dionysus.

102   Ariadne is the daughter of Minos, king of Crete. In the most common version,
      she helps the Athenian prince Theseus escape from the labyrinth at Cnossos and
      is taken by him to the island of Naxos. There he abandons her, but Dionysus finds
      and marries her. In Athens, on the second day (the "Choes" day) of the Anthesteria
      festival, the marriage of Ariadne and Dionysos was re-enacted; Ariadne was played
      by the wife of the archon basileus (the chief religious magistrate), and the god
      appeared either as a symbolic artifact or as a disguised man (or perhaps both).

103   The "painful ordeals" of Heracles are the tasks (usually twelve) he undertakes
      for Eurystheus, a punishment for having murdered his family while maddened
      by Hera. The marriage of Heracles and Youth, which presupposes Heracles'
      deification, is one of the most frequently-cited reasons (along with the mention of
      Latinus and the Etruscans in 1013-1016) for regarding the ending of the *Theogony*
      as written by someone later than Hesiod, since Heracles does not seem to be treated
      as a god before the sixth century.

she bore to him fine-ankled Medea, conquered
in love thanks to golden Aphroditė.[104]

[Children of the Goddesses]

Farewell now, you who have Olympian homes,
you islands, mainland, and salty sea within;
now, sweet-voiced Olympian Muses, daughters of   965
aegis-bearing Zeus, sing the tribe of goddesses,
immortals who went to bed with mortal men
and bore children similar to gods.

The divine goddess Demeter, joined in dear love
with the hero Iasius in a thrice-plowed field,   970
in the rich land of Crete, bore kindly Wealth,
who goes over the whole earth and the sea's wide
backs; who meets him and takes him in his arms,
the god makes rich and grants him much prosperity.[105]

Harmonia, daughter of golden Aphrodite, to Cadmus   975
bore Ino and Semele and fair-cheeked Agaue
and Autonoe, whom long-haired Aristaeus married,
and Polydorus in well-crowned Thebes.[106]

Callirhoe, Ocean's daughter, joined in golden
Aphrodite's love to strong-hearted Chrysaor,   980
bore a son, the strongest of all mortals,

---

104   The children of Helios (371) and Perseis (356) are Circe, the famous sorceress of the
       Odyssey, and Aeetes, king of Colchis and owner of the Golden Fleece at the time
       of the Argonauts' voyage. The daughter of Aeetes and the Oceanid Idyia (352) is
       Medea, who will marry Jason (1000) after helping him win the Fleece.

105   The union of Demeter and Iasius in a thrice-plowed field is mentioned by Homer
       (*Odyssey* 5.125-128) and must reflect a ritual practice intended to promote the
       fertility of the fields; this is why their son is Wealth (Plutus).

106   The children of Harmonia and Cadmus: the unfortunate Ino, wife of the Boeotian
       king Athamas, tried to kill her step-children and then killed her own son and
       herself (Apollodorus 1.9.1-2); transformed into the sea-goddess Leukothea, she
       gives an immortal veil to Odysseus in *Odyssey* 5.333-353. For Semele see on 940-
       942. Agaue is the mother of the Theban king Pentheus; in Euripides' *Bacchae*
       Pentheus is seduced by his enemy Dionysus into spying on the god's secret rites,
       whereupon the ecstatic Agaue mistakes her son for a lion and tears off his head.
       Aristaeus, a son of Apollo, and Autonoe are the parents of Acteon, who chances
       to see the goddess Artemis naked and is punished by being torn to pieces by his
       own hunting dogs. Polydorus is the father of Labdacus and great-grandfather of
       Oedipus (Euripides, *Phoenician Women* 7-9).

Geryoneus, whom forceful Heracles killed in
sea-swept Erythea for his rolling-gaited cattle.
    And Dawn bore to Tithonus bronze-crested Memnon,
king of the Ethiopians, and the lord Emathion.   985
And to Cephalus she bore a glorious son, valiant
Phaethon, a man like the gods; when he was young
in the delicate flower of famous youth, a child
of tender thoughts, laughter-loving Aphrodite
snatched him up and took and made him innermost   990
keeper of her holy temples, a godlike spirit.[107]
    Aeson's son, Jason, by the counsels of the eternal gods,
took from Aeetes, god-raised king, his daughter, Medea,
having finished the many painful ordeals
which the great and arrogant king assigned,   995
Pelias, violent and impetuous doer of wrong;
having finished these, Aeson's son came to Iolcus
after much labor, bringing the glancing girl
on the swift ship, and made her his fresh bride.
Mastered by Jason, shepherd of the people, she   1000
bore a son Medeus, whom Philyra's son Chiron
raised in the mountains; great Zeus' mind was done.[108]

---

107   The rapacious goddess Dawn (Eos), although married to Astraeus (378), is
continually carrying off other men; Apollodorus (1.4.4) says that her affair with
Ares angered Aphrodite, who caused her to be continually in love. Zeus granted
her request that Tithonus, a Trojan, be immortal, but she forgot to ask also that
he be ageless; finally he was reduced to a babbling and shriveled wreck (*Homeric
Hymn to Aphrodite* 218-238). Memnon, king of Troy's allies, the Ethiopians, is
killed in the Trojan War by Achilles, and Emathion is killed by Heracles during
his eleventh labor. The Athenian Cephalus was married to Procris, daughter of the
Athenian king Erechtheus before being carried off by Dawn

108   The "many painful ordeals" which Aeetes compels Jason to perform before he can
receive the Golden Fleece are, at least in later versions, accomplished for the most
part by Medea. Pelias is a "doer of wrong" because, among other crimes, he seized
the kingdom of Iolcus from Aeson, Jason's father and the rightful king. Upon
arriving in Iolcus, Medea tricks the daughters of Pelias into killing their father, thus
winning revenge for Jason just as she had won for him the Golden Fleece. Medeus,
the son of Jason and Medea, is the namesake of the Medes. Usually (as in Euripides'
Medea) the sons of Jason and Medea are killed by their mother to punish Jason, who
has left her for another woman, and Medeus is the son of Medea and Aegeus, king of
Athens and father of Theseus. Medeus is one of several heroes raised and educated
by the wise centaur Chiron in his famous cave on Mount Pelion.

As for the daughters of Nereus, old man of the sea,
the divine goddess Psamathe bore Phocus from the
love of Aeacus, thanks to golden Aphrodite;   1005
and the silver-shod goddess Thetis, mastered by Peleus,
bore Achilles, the lion-spirited manslayer.
    And well-crowned Cytherean Aphrodite bore Aeneas,
having joined in dear love with the hero Anchises
on the peaks of windy Ida with many glens.[109]   1010
    And Circe, daughter of the Sun, Hyperion's son,
in the love of patient-minded Odysseus bore
Agrius and Latinus, blameless and strong;
[and she bore Telegonus thanks to golden Aphrodite]
far away in a niche of holy islands   1015
they ruled over all the famous Tyrrhenians.[110]
    The divine goddess Calypso, joined to Odysseus
in dear love, bore Nausithoos and Nausinoos.[111]
    These are the immortals who went to bed with
mortal men and bore children similar to gods.   1020
Now, sweet-voiced Olympian Muses, daughters of
aegis-bearing Zeus, sing of the tribe of women.[112]

---

109   The affair of Aphrodite and the Trojan shepherd Anchises is told in the *Homeric Hymn to Aphrodite*. Zeus, blaming Aphrodite for the compulsion felt by himself and other gods to have sexual relations with mortals, inflicts a similar passion on the goddess; disguising herself as a mortal woman, she appears to Anchises, who falls in love and takes her to bed; afterwards the goddess reveals herself, announces that she will bear him a son Aeneas, and warns that Zeus will strike Anchises with lightning if he reveals her name. Aeneas is the famous hero of the foundation of Rome in the Roman poet Virgil's epic *Aeneid*.

110   Circe (957), the enchantress who turns Odysseus' men into animals in *Odyssey* 10, is usually the mother (and Odysseus the father) of Telegonus. Latinus is the legendary king of the Latins, whom Aeneas meets upon arriving in Italy, and the Tyrsenians are the Etruscans, the earliest historical inhabitants of Italy north of Rome. Although the author of 1015 seems to have little idea of the whereabouts of these peoples (somewhere in a "niche of holy islands"), knowledge of Latins and Etruscans, living somewhere to the west, must have been available in Greece during the second half of the 6th century.

111   Atlas' daughter Calypso (see on 359) is the nymph who keeps Odysseus in amiable servitude for seven years (*Odyssey* 7.244-263). She is childless in the *Odyssey*.

112   These two lines repeat 965-966 with only one word changed — "women" for "goddesses." A new subject is being introduced, with the Muses' help, and it must be the *Catalogue of Women*.

Introduction to *Works and Days*

The *Works and Days*, like the *Theogony*, originates in a tradition of oral poetry that began long before Hesiod. Like the *Theogony*, with its ties to Near Eastern succession myths, the *Works and Days* also has connections to the Near East, here to a tradition of "wisdom literature" that flourished in Asia Minor. And like the *Theogony* the *Works and Days* operates by bringing together various elements of its tradition in such a way as to bring out a single underlining meaning. In the *Theogony* Hesiod's material, the genealogies and stories of the gods, was relatively uniform and the poem's underlying theme, the coming to dominance of Zeus through both force and intelligence, was fairly direct. The *Works and Days* is in many ways more ambitious. Here Hesiod (assuming, as seems likely, that a single poet was responsible for the poem) has brought together myth, fable, personal experience, moral precepts, proverbs, agricultural advice, advice on sailing, what are to us superstitions about crossing rivers, cutting one's fingernails etc. and advice on lucky and unlucky days. In many ways the disparate nature of the evidence seems to be the point, since the underlying theme is how the will of Zeus informs all of human experience with a single underlying meaning.

The meaning itself is similar to that of Achilles' description in the *Iliad* of the two jars at Zeus' threshold, one of good, one of evils. From these Zeus sometimes gives human beings only evils, and sometimes evil mixed with good (24.527-33). We notice that Achilles leaves out the possibility that human beings might receive good unmixed with evil. This is also Hesiod's point: in looking at farming, in looking at human relations, in looking at economics or crossing rivers or the best days for being born or shearing sheep or getting married, for human beings there is no good without evil and no profit without hardship. Such is the will of Zeus for human beings in our present condition.

Justice in the *Works and Days*

The particular event that serves as a center for the *Works and Days* is a dispute over how to divide the farm left by their father to Hesiod and his brother Perses. The dispute may have been adjudicated by the local aristocracy in the marketplace of the nearest large town (probably Thespiae, although Hesiod never identifies it by name), a process depicted on Achilles' shield in the *Iliad* (18.497-508). All Hesiod says is that Perses unduly influenced the "gift-gobbling kings," as he calls them, and so got more than his fair share (37-41). The *Works and Days* is Hesiod's response. Here he demonstrates to both Perses and the kings that the gods have deliberately hidden man's livelihood from him (42) and that they do not mean human life to be easy. Thus, rather than simply having the earth provide food on its own, as it did in the golden age, Zeus has made it that men must work for a living. Similarly, Zeus holds out the prospect of great profit to be made by trading at sea, but only at the equally great risk of shipwreck. The myth of Prometheus illustrates the same lesson: Prometheus stole fire, a benefit for man, and Zeus countered by giving men an evil to match it. With neighbors, Hesiod points out, and with all human relations you only get out what you put in. There are hidden dangers in even minor acts, like resting the ladle on the mixing bowl or bathing, and while some days are unexpectedly propitious for a job, others are unexpectedly unlucky. Throughout human life, Hesiod seems to say, wherever you look, the message is the same: you can't get something for nothing.

Dikê or justice is the critical lesson that Hesiod draws from this in the *Works and Days*. If Perses and the kings could get away with their dishonesty they would have managed to gain profit without working for it. But Zeus does not allow this. Rather, as both proverbs and traditional wisdom inform us, Zeus brings evil to men who violate justice. Even more importantly, the tradition squares with Zeus' will as it is seen in the rest of human life. It is this larger context that saves the *Works and Days* from being mere moralism. Rather than merely repeating the tradition that Zeus punishes those who commit injustice, Hesiod shows that this must be true, since it is only one more manifestation of Zeus' universal will that human beings achieve no good without a balancing evil. Or as we might put it: no pain, no gain.

The message thus applies to a far wider audience than simply Perses and the kings, particularly since, as Hesiod's surprise reference to Perses' begging reveals (395-6), Perses has already learned the lesson. In short, the message applies to us. It is impossible for us to know whether an actual property dispute inspired the *Works and Days* or whether the poet created the case (and perhaps Perses as well) to suit his poem. Nor does it really matter. The aim of the *Works and Days* is to find within human life what the *Theogony* found within the divine order, an underlying meaning that unites the whole. Whether the poem was inspired by an actual or an imaginary lawsuit, the *Works and Days* accomplishes this end.

The Myths

Hesiod is quite explicit about the reason for introducing myth into the *Works and Days*: to show that human life is hard. He tells two myths, first that of Prometheus and Pandora and then the myth of the Five Ages. The myths seem, in terms of their content, to be contradictory (in the Prometheus myth, for example, sacrifice, fire, and women are introduced together, while they are divided in the scheme of the Five Ages). But both myths make the same point: Zeus does not mean human life to be easy. The myths, in this way, are not introduced as a "real" pre-history to human life, but rather because they illustrate, through two very different versions of that pre-history, the nature of human life now.

Pandora's name, "All-gift," sums up Hesiod's point. A gift looks like it is something for nothing. In fact, however, gifts require a payback, as Hesiod will make clear in showing how reciprocity runs throughout human relations (349-50, 354-5 etc.). In Pandora's case the gift comes, quite literally, with baggage. In the version of the Prometheus myth used in the *Theogony* Hesiod's interest is in Zeus' victory in cunning over Prometheus. Here the woman that Zeus gives as a return for fire is not named and brings with her no jar of troubles. In the *Works and Days*, where Hesiod's interest is what the story says about human life, the emphasis is on Pandora as a gift and on the jar. Both are revealed to be a mixture of good and evil. The woman is beautiful, but costly, and when Pandora removes the lid from the jar and the evils escape, Hope remains, fluttering under the lip of the jar. And even Hope can be both good and evil. It is an evil when we rely on it alone (as 455-7, 498-9), but in its other sense, as expectation, it is able to help human beings look past a present evil to a future good.

As the story of Prometheus illustrates, Hesiod's Zeus is not necessarily a beneficent deity. For Hesiod Zeus must be obeyed not because he is good, but because his will informs the cosmos. Zeus in this myth creates misery for mankind not because mankind deserves it, but because a offence committed by Prometheus ended up benefiting man. And lest we are tempted to trust too much in Zeus' good will, Hesiod shows him as laughing out loud at his ingenuity in making human life miserable (*WD* 59).

The Prometheus myth goes even further, illustrating not only the blend of good and evil in human life but also the particular way in which Zeus has made human life hard. Life is hard because it is never straight-forward: what looks good, like easy profit, turns out to bring disaster, while what looks bad, like hard work, turns out to be the only reliable good. Prometheus began this pattern in the *Theogony* by having Zeus choose between the bad part of the sacrifice, hidden in a good exterior, and the good part, hidden in a bad exterior (*Th.* 535-57). The myth explains why humans eat the meat from the sacrifice while the gods get only the bones. In Hesiod's version it also sets up Zeus' retaliation with the woman, who, in the *Works and Days,* is beautiful on the outside but hides "the heart of a thief" within (*WD* 67, 78). Prometheus, whose name means "Forethought," had warned his brother about gifts from Zeus. But Epimetheus, "Afterthought," is fooled by the lovely exterior. Like the fool, Perses, he only learns by suffering (218): "and then when he had the evil, he knew it" (89).

Obeying Zeus' will, for Hesiod, is not merely a matter of obedience and self-restraint. It is also, and equally, necessary to understand it, and Zeus does not make this easy. Nor is negotiating one's way in the world a simple matter. The *Works and Days* is full of things that, like Pandora, are both good and bad, shame (317-9), neighbors (346-7), wives (702-5), hope (498-9), generosity (356, 364-5), talk (760-4) and the quality that opens the poem, strife (11 ff.). As with Pandora, or as with the specious good of stolen profit, it is dangerous to be taken in by appearances. Knowing when, how, and how much is crucial (694). As Hesiod says, with a hit at Perses: "a man who himself does not know and, hearing another, / will not take it to heart, that man is useless completely." (296-7)

The myth of the Five Ages is introduced after the Prometheus myth as "another account" (*logos*) (106) of "how men and gods came from the same source" (108). Hesiod's perhaps over-emphatic wish to have been born earlier or later than his own time, the iron age (174-5), may imply that the myth originally portrayed a cycle of ages, from gold to iron and then back to gold. As Hesiod uses the myth, however, what it illustrates is degeneration, from gold, to silver, to bronze to finally iron. As the gods are said to "make" each of the successive generations, gods and men "come from one source" only in that both once lived without need. And as the myth traces the gradual introduction of need into human life, it also introduces what we often call civilization. This development appears most clearly in the cities, ships and armies that enter into the world with the age of the heroes, an age that Hesiod has inserted into the original metallic scheme. What could have been composed as a myth of progress (as in the *Prometheus Bound* 437 ff.) is thus conceived as a myth of degeneration. Like the Prometheus myth, it shows how first "the gods" (109-10, 127-9) and then Zeus (143-4, 157-9, 180-1) have willed that human life be difficult.

The conclusion of the myth of the Five Ages, with its picture of the departure of Shame (*aidos*) and Nemesis (retribution) from the earth, returns the poem to the theme of justice, as the Prometheus myth of the *Theogony,* for example, both begins and ends with the chains Zeus uses to bind Prometheus (*Th.* 521-2, 613-6). This A B A (or expanded, A B C B A) structure, often called a "ring pattern," is common in oral poetry. Hesiod uses it to mark off the larger units of his poem, to emphasize the primary theme of a section, and to connect the section with what follows. The return to the theme of justice here connects the myths to the fable of the hawk and the nightingale, in which Hesiod describes for the kings what it is to be caught by a higher power. The fable, which has been interpreted both as showing Hesiod in the clutches of the kings and as showing the kings in the clutches of the higher power of Zeus, may in fact illustrate both. Hesiod's Zeus is ruthless. The kings may for a while take over Zeus' role, but soon, as Hesiod is about to make clear, they will experience his power – and in a way they will not particularly like.

Farming

A long section describing the farmer's year, which includes trading by sea, dominates the second half of the *Works and Days* and a section on lucky and unlucky days closes the poem. But while the title "Works and Days" (*Erga kai Hemerai*) appears to have been given in reference to these sections in particular it also suits the poem as a whole. "Works" (*erga*) are both human deeds, discussed in the first half of the poem, and the fields men plow, "the works" as Hesiod says "of the oxen and the laboring mules" (46) discussed in the second half. The days also are both the lucky and unlucky days and the days for each job in its season, a seasonableness that Hesiod stresses in his description both of farming and of proper behavior. Timing, for Hesiod, is all. On the farm the need for perception and quickness comes in knowing the days for each work and being able to read the pattern of the seasons set in the constellations and marked by the plants, trees, birds and animals whose lives move with the seasons. The task is not an easy one, for while the pattern is regular, it is also complicated by Zeus' shifting ways with the weather and by the lucky and unlucky days that also "come from Zeus" (765, 769).

The farming section of the *Works and Days*, although it has been regarded as a manual or set of instructions, teaches almost nothing about farming that an ordinary sixth-century country person would not already know. Moreover, the detail which opens the section, about how long to make the axle for a wagon or how much bread a plowman should get for his lunch, soon gives way to a vivid, impressionistic, and highly manipulated description of how the year feels to the farmer. Although the *Works and Days* looks to many sources for its clues to the will of Zeus, its primary evidence is here, in the experience that Hesiod recreates of working with the seasons as Zeus sends them. The vivid depiction of the farmer's year, with its balance of winter against summer, hardship against plenty, and labor against leisure, itself illustrates the balance of good and evil that Hesiod finds in human life. But even more significantly, there is a noumenal quality to working the land. This world, for Hesiod, is full of gods.

Here, as throughout, it is critical to remember that if Hesiod wrote, he wrote only in what we term capital letters. That is, he did not distinguish in his writing, as a modern text must, between Earth the goddess and earth as it is plowed, between Justice the daughter of Zeus and justice as judged by the kings, or between Strife the daughter of Night and the strife of his own quarrel with Perses. The omnipresence of the divine that this gives rise to appears in the *Works and Days'* quite unusual depiction of the gods. Three gods occupy the center of the poem, Zeus, Justice and Demeter, goddess of the harvest. The other Olympians, such as Athena, Poseidon, Hera, Dionysus or Hermes, are mentioned only in passing or not at all. In their place the more noumenal forces, the rivers and sun, the constellations, the winds, even rumor, inform Hesiod's world. And at the center of these, informing and ordering, is Zeus and the seasons that set all the elements of the farmer's world in their yearly cycle of change and interaction.

The importance of the seasons to Hesiod, evident in the *Works and Days'* continual injunction to work "in season," also appears at the end of the *Theogony*. Here, as Hesiod describes how Zeus begot his new order into the cosmos, the Seasons take pride of place, before even the Fates who are also daughters of Zeus by Themis, "Right." Their significance appears in the highly unusual names Hesiod gives them, not "Summer," "Winter" and "Spring" nor, as in Athens, "Flourishing" and "Fruitfulness" (Pausanias 9.35.1) but rather Good-governance or Lawfulness (*Eunomia*), Justice (*Dikê*), and Peace (*Eirene*). Hesiod explains that the Seasons (*Horae*) "care for (*horeuousi*) the works / fields of men who are mortal" (903). The pun, as well as the association of the natural seasons which govern the fields (*erga*) with the political forces of Good-order, Justice and Peace that order the deeds (also *erga*) of human beings, reflects the association of justice and farming made in the *Works and Days*. More importantly, perhaps, it reflects Hesiod's sense that the same will of Zeus informs every part of the world about him, most evidently on the farm. This is nowhere more true than in the distinction which opens the *Works and Days*, between bad Strife, which causes war, violence, and cheating, and good Strife which gives rise to competition, and which Zeus has set "in the roots of the earth" (19). Although there are, as Hesiod has discovered, two kinds of strife, one that appears in striving to take other men's goods and the other that appears in striving to gain a living from the earth, they are also, in an even more fundamental way, two sides of a single quality.

The *Works and Days* represents Hesiod as a small farmer in the backwoods of Boeotia (about 60 miles northwest of Athens, traveling over Mount Cithaeron). The Muses' gift of poetry depicted in the *Theogony* (22-34) could well describe a young man who discovered in himself, in the lonely hours herding sheep, a talent for the oral poetry he had grown up hearing at festivals and, perhaps, in the marketplace. As with all the details of Hesiod's life, we cannot know for sure. It is impossible even for us to know if there was such a person as "Hesiod" and if there was, whether or not he composed both the *Theogony* and the *Works and Days*, as the *Works and Days* implies (658-60). Whatever Hesiod's status, however, the *Works and Days* gives us a vivid sense of how the world looked in the sixth century B.C.. It also lets us listen to a very particular voice. It is a voice that takes in equally myth, proverb, fable, superstition (from our point of view) and a strong personal distaste for the sea. It is marked by a distinct streak of misogyny, a distrust of the elite, a feeling that heroic values are out of date, and a loathing of violence. It is a harsh voice, insistent on hard work and the demands of the gods, but it is also aware of the life of the young woman "unlearned yet in the works of golden Aphrodite" (521). It is an unforgiving voice, but also a surprisingly personal one. It is deeply imbued with the traditional language of oral poetry but also wonderfully given to sportive coinages: the robber as the "day-sleeper" (605); the snail as the "house-carrier" (571) and even an octopus as "the boneless one" (524). And finally the voice is marked by a deep sensitivity to the rhythms of the year, to the ways of the birds and animals that share the world of the farm with human beings, and to the need to look deeper into the cosmos as it manifests itself about us. The voice may or may not be that of a small farmer from Boeotia named Hesiod, but it is a unique voice and one well worth listening to nonetheless.

In the translation which follows, for ease of comparison with other translations, the line numbers follow the original Greek rather than my English translation. I have remained as close as possible to the Greek while attempting to capture Hesiod's unique diction, which moves seamlessly between the quite down to earth and even mundane and the high epic style he shares with Homer. In the few cases where I have rephrased the Greek, I include a footnote giving the literal translation. For the sake of the rhythm of the lines I have allowed myself some liberties with the formal epithets that Hesiod shares with the oral tradition, so that "cloud-gathering Zeus," for example, occasionally becomes simply "Zeus" or "Hermes, slayer of Argus" simply "Hermes." I have also, for the convenience of the reader, glossed a number of Hesiod's references in the text, so that Hesiod's "the lame god," has become "Hephaistus, the lame god" and "Notus" "Notus, the south wind." With more hesitation I have also glossed Hesiod's coinages, so that his plain "the house-carrier" has become "the snail, house-carrier" or the "the wise one" "the ant, the wise one" etc.. I have bracketed the headings of the sections to remind the reader that these are my invention and not Hesiod's. Lines bracketed within the text have been condemned by some editors as later additions. And finally, as Hesiod is quite clear that his imagined audience is primarily male, I have not hesitated to use "man" and "men" for "human beings".

Stephanie Nelson

Works and Days

[Prologue]¹

Muses who dwell on Pieria², you who, through song, give glory,
come, speak of Zeus, hymn your father, through whom mortal men
are known and unknown, famous, forgotten, at the will of great Zeus.   5
For with ease he makes a man strong and gives a strong man over to hardship,
and with ease he dims the great and makes the obscure bright,
and with ease he straightens the crooked and withers the mighty,
Zeus who thunders on high, who dwells at home in the highest.
Hear, see, and attend, and through justice keep our law righteous –
for your part. For mine, I would speak truth to Perses.   10
                                        There is not, it turns out,
only one kind of Strife; rather, over the earth, there are two.³
The first someone would praise when he knew her, the second's
worth blame; their natures are different, completely. The one
fosters war, that evil, and quarrels and contests, the hard-hearted one.
Her no man would be close to; it is by necessity,   15
through the design of the gods, men honor this strife, this burden.
But the other, the first born, the child of dark Night,
Zeus, son of Cronus, high-throned, who dwells in brightness,
set in the roots of the earth, and for men she is better.
It is she who stirs an unhandy man, even him, to start working,   20
for one man watches another and feels then a longing for work,

---

1   Headings are placed in brackets because they have been added by the translator.
     Lines bracketed in the text have been thought by some editors to be later additions
     to the poem. For ease of cross-reference, the line numbers follow those of the
     Greek text rather than of the translation.

2   Pieria, north of Mount Olympus in Thessaly, had a well-known cult of the Muses.
     Theogony 53 identifies Pieria as the Muses' birthplace

3   In the *Theogony* Night gives birth to a single Strife (Eris) (*Th.* 225) who goes on to
     bear a long list of evil abstractions. Hesiod's "so it turns out" (*ara*) seems to be a
     deliberate reference to this passage.

when he looks at a rich man, who hastens to plow and sow
and set his household in order; so neighbor envies his neighbor
as he hastens towards wealth – for this strife is a good one for mortals –
and potter is rival to potter and craftsman to craftsman   25
and beggar is jealous of beggar, and poet of poet.

[Perses and the Kings]

Perses, set these things in store in your heart; don't let the Strife
who relishes evil keep your heart back from work, with you looking
after quarrels in the marketplace, a listener-in and a cheat.
The season for quarrels is short, and care for the marketplace,   30
when the year's living is yet to be stored, inside in the barn
in its season – the living the earth bears, the grain of Demeter.
When you have plenty of that, go on with your quarrels, disputing
after other men's goods. But you'll get no second chance
for that work. So come, let us settle our quarrel instead, right now   35
with straight judgments; straight judgments are from Zeus and the best.
For already we had divided the farm, but you kept on grabbing,
carrying off the most of it, feeding the kings with great glory,
gift-gobblers, who like judging this kind of justice.
Idiots. They don't know that the half is more than the whole   40
nor what is good about mallow and asphodel.[4]

[Prometheus and Pandora] [5]

For the gods have hidden
our livelihood and hold it from us. Otherwise, easily, you could work
for a day and have enough for a year and do no more work.
You could put the boat's rudder up over the fireplace in the smoke   45

---

4   The advantage of mallow and asphodel appears to be that it is poor fare (asphodel
     grows freely in the underworld, as *Odyssey* 11.523) and so is not grudged by the
     gods, much like the "half" which is therefore better than the whole. See the
     Introduction, pp. 63-64, for this theme and for Hesiod's quarrel with his brother
     Perses. The word "idiot" here (*nepios*) is elsewhere translated "fool." See n. 13.

5   In the *Theogony* version of this myth Hesiod presents the theft of fire as the
     second stage in Prometheus' challenge of Zeus, which begins with the division
     of the sacrifice. Prometheus' name means "Fore-thought" as contrasted, in this
     version, to his brother Epimetheus, or "After-thought." See the *Theogony* 521-616
     for parallels to this story, as well as the Introduction, pp. 65-66. *Bios*, translated as
     "livelihood" below, can also mean simply "life."

and let the works of the oxen go hang, and of the long-laboring mules.[6]
But Zeus hid it, enraged in his heart because crooked-minded Prometheus
tricked him. And so for men Zeus plotted grief and trouble.
He hid fire. And Prometheus, bold son of Iapetus, stole it back   50
from the side of wise Zeus, in a fennel stalk, and gave it to men
and Zeus who delights in the thunder did not notice.
So in anger Zeus spoke to him, Zeus, who gathers the clouds:
        "Son of Iapetus, all-cunning, wily in plots,
you delight in your stealing of fire and in outwitting me –   55
it will be a plague, a great one, to you, and to men to come.
I too will give them a gift, an evil one, answering fire,
in which all will delight in their hearts, as they embrace their own evil."
        So he spoke, and laughed, the father of gods and men.
And he ordered famous Hephaestus, as quick as he could,   60
to mix earth with water, and to put in a human voice
and human strength and make the face like a goddess immortal
and shape a maiden's most beautiful form. And Zeus bid Athena
to teach her her works – how to weave the varied, intricate web –
and he told Aphrodite, the golden, to pour grace around her   65
and hard longing and knee-weakening care; and he told Hermes
to put in the mind of a bitch and the heart of a thief,
Hermes the guide, the messenger, and the slayer of Argus.[7]
        So he spoke; and they obeyed him, lord Zeus, Cronus' son.
Right away Hephaestus, the famous lame god, formed from earth   70
one like a revered, modest maiden, as was Cronus' son great counsel.
And bright-eyed Athena, goddess, clothed and adorned her
and the Graces, bright goddesses, and the lady Persuasion
put gold adornments on her, and the Horae, the lovely-haired
Seasons, crowned her with flowers of springtime,   75
[and all her ornaments Pallas Athena shaped to her body.]
And then Hermes, the slayer of Argus, the guide, put into her breast

---

6   As below (l. 629) the rudder is hung up over the fireplace so that the smoke will
     preserve it.

7   Hephaestus, the blacksmith and god of fire, is also the god of crafts and so of
     anything "man-made." Athena is a goddess not only of war and intelligence (as
     Theogony 924-6) but also of weaving, the essential work of a woman. Hermes is a
     god of boundaries and also of violating boundaries, hence his role as a messenger
     and his association with theft. In the *Homeric Hymn to Hermes* for example, while
     still a baby, Hermes steals Apollo's cattle. See also the note on *Theogony* 938-9.

lies and wheedling words and the heart of a thief,
[fashioned at the plan of loud-thundering Zeus, and speech]
the gods' herald placed in her too, and he gave this one, the woman,   80
a name – Pandora, "All-gift," since the gods on Olympus
gave her all as a gift, a bane to men who eat bread.[8]
    But when the deceit, sheer and without cure, was finished,
Zeus the father sent Hermes, Argus' slayer, the gods' famed messenger
to Epimetheus, Afterthought, bearing the gift.   85
And Epimetheus never thought of what his brother, Prometheus, had told him:
to take no gift from Olympian Zeus, but send it right back
lest it turn out some kind of evil for men. So Epimetheus took it,
and then, when the evil was his, knew what it was.
                            For before this human tribes
had lived on the land clear of evils, distant from harsh toil   90
and pain and diseases, the givers of doom to men
[since mortal men grow old quickly in evil and hardship.]
But the woman took the great lid of the jar in her hands
and scattered them, and contrived grief and trouble for humans.   95
Only Hope stayed inside there, in its unbreakable home,
under the lip of the jar – for she threw back the lid
before Hope flew out the door; so willed great cloud-gathering Zeus.
    But ten thousand other afflictions wander among us;   100
the earth has its fill of evils, and the sea is full, and sicknesses
come by day to men and by night, roaming at will,
bringing their evils in silence – for Zeus, the wise-minded,
took out their voices.[9] So there is no way at all to avoid Zeus' mind.   105

[The Five Ages]

    And, if you like, there is another account; I can sum it up
well and with knowledge, and you store it deep in your heart –
how mortal men and the gods came to be from one source.
Golden were the first kind of men who could speak,

---

8   The line could mean either that all the gods gave a gift to Pandora, or that they all
       gave her as a gift to men. I have tried to keep my translation ambiguous. In this
       version Pandora brings with her a jar of evils (which could themselves be the gods'
       gifts) while in the *Theogony* version Pandora herself is the evil that Zeus send to
       men. See the Introduction, p. 65.
9   Since Zeus removed the voices from the diseases, human beings cannot hear them
       coming and so cannot protect themselves.

made by the undying gods who live on Olympus;   110
they lived in Cronus' time, while he was king of high heaven.[10]
These men lived like the gods; their hearts had no trouble;
toil and sorrow were far from them. Old age and its wretchedness
did not come upon them; they rejoiced in abundance
with arms and legs never weakened, out of the reach of all evil.[11]   110
They died as if conquered by sleep, and all that is good
was theirs. The fertile plowland brought them crops without stinting
— in plenty all on its own. They tended their fields as they pleased,
at ease and at peace in abundance; their blessings were many.
They were rich in flocks and close to the gods who are happy.   120
        But when earth covered over this kind –
who are spirits over the land, through great Zeus' designs,[12]
kindly, warding off evil, guardians for mortal men, keeping close watch
over judgments and pitiless deeds, clothed in mist, everywhere roaming   125
over the land, and givers of wealth, for this kingly prize was theirs too –
then the gods on Olympus made another, a second kind,
one made of silver and worse, not like the gold in body or mind.
A hundred years a child stayed by the side of his lady mother,
a great infant,[13] being raised and skipping about in the house.   130
Then, when they were grown and had come to the measure of youth,
through their folly they lived short lives full of pain.
For they could not hold back from wrong; they outraged one another;

---

10   The time of Cronus, Zeus' father, is traditionally associated with a Golden Age, as
      here, just as in Italy Saturn was associated with a time before violence and injustice
      and before human beings were forced to work. Zeus enters into Hesiod's scheme
      when he, as opposed to "the gods," is said to destroy the second, Silver, age and
      create the third, the Bronze (138, 143). Hesiod calls each stage a *genos*, "kind" or
      "race" or "age," but does not see one as descended from another. Since the gods are
      said to "make" the men of each age, Hesiod's statement that "mortal men and the
      gods came to be from one source" (108) must mean that men and gods at first lived
      similarly, before hardship came into human life. Plato will adapt this myth in the
      Republic (415 a-b, and 547a) to portray the different kinds of citizens in his city.
      See also the Introduction, page 66.

11   Literally, "with hands and feet always the same."

12   This is the manuscript reading. In the *Cratylus* Plato quotes the line rather
      differently: "who are called blessed spirits upon the land." "Spirits" here is
      daimones, often seen as a kind of intermediary between the human and the divine.

13   "Infant" (etymologically, "not-speaking") is a literal gloss of Hesiod's word *nepios*,
      which elsewhere in the poem is translated as "fool" or "idiot."

they would not serve the immortals nor sacrifice on their altars,   135
which for humans, by custom, is right.[14] So Zeus, son of Cronus,
hid them in his anger, since they would not give honor to the gods
who, blessed, hold Mt. Olympus.
                          But when earth had covered these too –   140
who are called the mortal and blessed ones under the earth,
a second kind of protector, but they have their honor as well[15] –
then Zeus the father created another, a third kind of men of clear speech,
a bronze race, not like the silver, of ash trees,[16]
mighty and terrible. Their only care was the works of the war god,   145
groans, outrage, and insolence; they did not eat bread
and the strong hearts in their breasts were of adamant. Their huge force
was unapproachable. Ungraspable hands
reached from the strong arms of their shoulders.
Their weapons, their houses, were bronze; their work was with bronze–   150
they had no black iron.[17] And they, mastered by their own hands,
went down to cold Hades' home in the shadows,
nameless, taken, for all of their terrible power,   155
by dark death, and they left the bright light of the sun.
     But when the land had covered this kind too, Zeus, Cronus' son,
made another on the nourishing land, a fourth kind, more just and better,
of heroes like gods, men called half-gods – the race before ours   160
over the unmeasured earth.[18] And of these, cruel war and the battle cry

---

14   *Kata ethea*, "according to custom," could also mean "according to their location /
      usual place."

15   These spirits may be identified with the cults of heroes who, like Oedipus at the end
      of Sophocles' *Oedipus at Colonus*, were worshipped as powers guarding the area
      around their burial place.

16   Hesiod may mean that the race was born from the ash-tree nymphs (the Meliae,
      Theogony 187), or the reference may be, as often, to ash-tree spears.

17   Hesiod here links his overall scheme of degenerating metals to what is still known
      as the "Bronze Age," the period before the discovery of iron. The heroes celebrated
      by Homer, whom Hesiod places in the next generation, traditionally used bronze,
      but also possessed iron, as *Iliad* 23.826-9, and *Odyssey* 1.184.

18   Literally, "the earlier race." Here, as in his abrupt introduction of his own age,
      the iron age, Hesiod blurs over the fact that the aristocracy of his own time traced
      their descent back to the heroes. He seems to want each "kind" to be considered
      separately. Oedipus, along with heroes such as Heracles or Jason, was traditionally
      of the older generation of heroes while the heroes of Troy, Achilles, Agamemnon,
      Odysseus, etc. were of the younger generation.

destroyed some, some under Thebes' seven gates in Cadmus' land,
fighting for Oedipus' flocks, and some went in ships
and crossed the great gulf of the sea to Troy to fight for fair Helen.   165
There, for some, the end that is death enfolded them,
while for others Zeus, Cronus' son, gave custom and livelihood far from
                                                                    mankind,
a living at the edge of the earth, and the father settled them there.
And there they live, by deep-flowing Ocean on isles of the blessed –   170
heroes, and happy, with hearts free from care, for whom the grain-giving
                                                                    plowland
bears crops thrice yearly, abundant and honey-rich.[19]
                                        But for the fifth –
I wish I had never been born in this age, but either died first   175
or been born after. For the age now is iron, and neither by day
can men rest from labor and sorrow, nor by night, as they perish away,
and the gods will give more harsh trouble.
                                Yet, all the same, for these
some good will be mixed with the evil. But Zeus will destroy them,
                                                this race   180
of men with clear speech, when the children are born with grey heads.
Then a father will fight with his children, children with their fathers,
a guest will fight with his host, and comrade with comrade,
and brothers will no longer be close, as once they were.
Parents, unhonored, blamed and reproached, will quickly grow old;   185
hard children will give them hard words, knowing no fear of the gods,
and when they grow old will grudge to give back their rearing,
manhandling justice.[20] One man will ravage another man's city;
no thanks and no grace for keeping of oaths,   190
none for a just man or a good one; they honor a man who does evil
and praise outrage. Their justice lies in their hands; shame and respect
will be gone. A bad man will harm his better with false speeches

---

19   Two papyri preserve some fragmentary lines, 173a-d, which may have been added
      to parallel the earlier generations: "far from the immortals. And for them Cronus
      is king / whom the father of men and of gods released from his chains / and now,
      among these, he has always his honor, as is right. / Then Zeus made yet another
      kind of men with clear speech / of those who live now upon the earth that feeds
      many."

20   Literally: "hand-justicers" a condensed version of "justice (lies) in their hands", l.
      192 below.

and swear an oath to affirm them. Envy will be men's companion,   195
harsh-worded, delighting in evil and hateful, and men will have misery.
And then, their forms covered in white, forsaking mankind
for Olympus to be with the gods, away from the wide paths of the land,
will go Retribution and Shame[21] – and what will be left for men   200
is bitter pain, and no help against evil.

[The Hawk and the Nightingale] [22]

And now I will tell a tale for the kings, who know it themselves,
how a hawk, high in the clouds, spoke to a nightingale
clutching the speckle-necked bird, as he carried her off in his claws;
she wailed, pierced by the hooks of his nails,   205
but he gave speech in his strength: "Strange one, why do you cry?
One greater than you now has you. You will go where I take you,
singer though you are – a dinner for me, if I wish, or I may let you go.
Only a fool stands up to oppose the stronger;   210
he loses his victory, has that disgrace, and more – he has pain as well."
So he spoke, the hawk of swift flight, the long-winged bird.

[Justice and the Kings]

So Perses, you listen to justice; don't breed outrage and insult.[23]
Outrage is an evil for a poor man; not even a great one can carry it lightly
when he meets with ruin – then he bows down under its weight.[24]   215
The road to travel lies on the other side – the better road, the one to justice.
At the end justice is strong over outrage, the lesson a fool learns
by suffering. For Oath runs alongside crooked judgments,

---

21   *Aidos* (Shame, and above, at line 192, translated as "shame and respect") is the
      force that keeps men from doing wrong out of respect for the opinions of others.
      Nemesis (Retribution or Righteous Indignation) is the anger men feel at injustice
      whether or not they themselves are the victims. See also the note on *Theogony* 223.

22   The usual interpretation of this fable is that the nightingale, a singer, represents
      Hesiod and the hawk represents the kings. It is also possible, however, that the
      nightingale represents the kings who are themselves in the grip of a higher power,
      that of Zeus. See the Introduction, p. 67. "Strange one" below translates *daimonie*,
      otherwise "divine one."

23   "Outrage and insult" here, as "outrage" in the next line translates the Greek word
      hubris which, between human beings, implies a failure to respect the integrity, or
      in the modern concept, "rights," of another.

24   "Ruin" (Greek *atê*) here as at line 231 also has connotations of the destruction or
      blind infatuation that results from overweening pride, as *Iliad* 9.504.

and when men haul Justice about, forcing her to go where she's dragged,
there's a commotion – gift-gobblers, men who judge right with bent justice. 220
Then Justice follows mourning the city and customs of the people
clothed in mist, bringing evil where men drove her out and dealt her
not straightly.[25]

        But where men give straight judgments   225
to strangers and citizens, where they do not step outside justice,
they prosper; their city prospers; and the people blossom within it.
Peace is a nurse to their children. There far-seeing Zeus never
marks out war's pain. Famine is no companion to them, nor ruin,[26]   230
but straight in their justice, in abundance, they care for well-tended
fields. The earth gives them livelihood. The mountain oaks,
high in the branches, bear acorns; in the trunks the bees have their hives;
their sheep are heavy with fleeces; their children look like their fathers.   235
They flourish with good things throughout and do not sail on ships,
and the grain-giving plowland bears them crops.

        But for those given to
outrage, evil, and hard-hearted deeds, for them far-seeing Zeus marks a
judgment. And often a whole city suffers for one evil man,   240
presumptuous, who contrives evil. On them, from the sky, Zeus brings calamity,
famine together with plague; the people die off; no children
are born to the women; the households diminish – all through
the contriving of Olympian Zeus. And then, at another time,   245
he destroys their wide army or their walls, or else Cronus' son
plucks off their ships on the sea.

        You kings, take heed; mark for yourselves
this judgment. For immortals, close-by, note your crooked judgments   250
where men wear down one another, blind to the wrath of the gods.
Thrice ten thousand immortals guard mortal men, watchers
for Zeus over the flourishing land; they are guardians of judgments

---

25   Throughout this passage, and Hesiodic poetry overall, there is no strict division
    between personifications, such as Oath and Justice, and the entities they represent.
    The capital letters introduced here to distinguish personifications were not used in
    ancient Greek texts. See the Introduction, pp. 67-68.

26   "Ruin" translates atê, as in note 24 above. The tradition of the earth flourishing
    under a just king appears as well in *Odyssey* 19.109-14, while the plague and
    infertility which strike as a result of unpunished murder features prominently in
    the *Oedipus Tyrannus*. There is also, of course, a pragmatic relation between a
    sound political condition and the flourishing of agriculture, as implied at *Theogony*
    901-3, for which see the Introduction, p. 68.

and hard-hearted deeds, clothed in mist, roaming the land.   255
And there is Justice, a maiden, the child of great Zeus. She has renown
and reverance from the gods. When a man's crooked scorn
does her harm, she sits down by Zeus, her father, Cronus' son,
and speaks about men's unjust minds. Then a people pay back   260
the kings' insolence, kings who, thinking ruin, turned their judgments aside
and spoke crookedly. Keep watch over this; keep your words straight, you kings,[27]
you gift-gobblers – and forget everything about crooked judgments.

    A man sets up evil for himself when he sets up evil for others;   265
the evil design is worst for the one who designed it.[28]

    The eye of Zeus, that sees all, knows all, surveying all things,
sees this too if he wishes; it does not escape him
what kind of justice this is in the city.

                             Nor would I myself   270
now be just among men, nor want my son to be just,
since justice is an evil where good things go for injustice[29] –
but I don't expect, yet, that wise Zeus will bring that to pass.

    And you Perses, you store these things up in your mind,
you listen to justice – and forget about force altogether.   275
For this is the way men are to live;[30] this is what Zeus has ordained,
that for fish and for beasts and for swift-flighted birds,[31]
they eat one another, since they have no justice among them.
But to men he gave justice, and that, in the end, is the best.
For if someone knows what he says and willingly speaks what is right,   280
to him Zeus, the far-seeing, gives wealth. But if someone bears witness,
swears an oath, and deliberately lies, he harms justice,
a wrong without cure – and feeble and dim generations are left to his house.
But for the man who swears truth, the generations after are better.   285

---

27   Other manuscripts read "keep straight your judgments".

28   Here, as often, Hesiod rounds off specific advice by citing what appear to be
       proverbs that demonstrate his point.

29   Hesiod puns here on *dikê*, which can mean "justice," "judgment" or even (as line
       239) "punishment." Literally the line reads: "if the more unjust man will have the
       greater justice / judgment (*dikê*)".

30   "Way" here translates *nomos*, which also means "custom," and later "law," as well
       as the characteristic "way" of a group. At *Theogony* 74, Zeus is said to give to the
       immortals their "ways" (*nomos*) and honors (*timê*).

31   The reference to birds here has been taken as a comment on the fable of 202-12. If
       the fable there identifies the kings with the hawks this line would then point out
       that human beings should not behave similarly.

[Reciprocity and Hard Work]

To you then, Perses, fool though you are, I will speak with fair thought.
Evil is easy to take; crowds come upon her; the road is smooth
and she lives close by. But excellence, the gods put sweat before that;   290
the path that leads there is long; that road is steep
and at first rough. When you come to the top, then it starts
to come easier, but it's hard all the same.
                                        That man is best,
altogether, who thinks things through for himself – who figures
what will be best later on and finally.
Someone who can listen is good too; he hears when someone speaks well. 295
But a man who won't listen and knows nothing himself,
who takes nothing to heart, he is useless.
                                        But for you,
keep what I tell you in mind: work, Perses, work,
you offspring of Zeus; make famine hate you; make   300
Demeter your friend. Then she, revered with rich crowns,
will stuff full your barn with livelihood, for famine
is the constant companion of one who won't work. Nemesis
follows such men, men the gods hate and men hate, a man who won't work,
like the drone, with no sting, wasting the hive's labor, idle,   305
and eating.
                                        But you rather, prize the work; arrange it in measure;
make your barns, in their season, full of livelihood.
Men's flocks prosper from work; work makes men rich;
and you will be close to the undying gods, much more
if you work, [and to men, for they hate the unworking].   310
Work is no shame; not working is the disgrace.
Work, and envy will come soon enough from the idle,
and admiration, as you grow rich; fame and excellence attend on wealth.[32]
Whatever your lot, work is best, if you can manage
to turn your witless mind from other men's goods   315
back to your work, and, as I tell you, care for your living.

---

32   "Excellence" (*aretê*) also "status" or "virtue," is the primary goal of the Homeric
      hero, whose heroic values Hesiod seems here to be undermining by associating
      them primarily with wealth. "Admire and envy" translates *zelos*, the complex of
      feelings that comes from looking at someone above oneself. "Lot," below, translates
      daimon, otherwise "spirit" or "fortune."

Shame is no good at looking after a man who is needy,[33]
shame is a great harm to men, and a great benefit too –
shame leads to no great prosperity; boldness goes with wealth.
   Property is not there to be grabbed; what is better is god-given.   320
A man can take wealth by force, with a strong hand,
or steal with his tongue, as often, when gain
tricks a man's mind and shamelessness tramples his shame,
but then easily the gods blot him out, bring down his household,   325
and wealth, his valet, soon leaves his service.
It is the same to injure a guest-friend, or to do evil
to a man at your mercy,[34] or climb up into your brother's bed
and lie with his wife, doing in secret an act out of season,
or if some fool offends against fatherless children,   330
or when his father is old, on that evil threshold,
gives him abuse, quarreling with harsh words – with him
Zeus is angry; and Zeus himself in the end
imposes a rough exchange as the price of those unjust deeds.
   But you, hold off your witless heart from these things   335
and, where you can, sacrifice as is due to the deathless gods
pure and clear, and kindle the gleaming thigh-bones. Other times
have libations and incense appease them, when you lie down to sleep
and when the holy light comes, so they may see you with kindness
and have a heart that is gracious, and you buy the farm of another   340
and not have another buy yours.[35]
               Call your friend to a feast; leave an enemy be.[36]
Most of all invite the man who lives nearest; since if something is wrong
on the place, neighbors come as they are – in-laws take time to dress.   345
A bad neighbor is a plague, just as much as a good one is a gain.
To have a good one to your share is to have a share in distinction

---

33   An alternative reading would give "A not good shame looks after a needy man."

34   These are the classic offenses punished by Zeus himself, in particular injuring a
     suppliant (here "a man at your mercy") or a guest-friend. Hesiod's point is that
     stealing money is an offense just as bad as these.

35   As money was not yet used in Hesiod's Ascra one would acquire the allotment of
     another by exchange of goods, probably by having someone gradually borrow so
     much that the only way to settle was to give over his land. The translation gives a
     modern equivalent.

36   To regard others as either "friends" (*philoi*) or "enemies" (*echthroi*), that is, as
     either one's own people or not one's own people, is common in the Greek tradition.
     Elsewhere, as lines 15, 184 etc. I translate "be friendly" as "be close to."

already.[37] If you had no bad neighbors your cattle would never be lost.[38]
From your neighbor, then, take fair measure and pay back
in the same measure, what is fair; pay him back with more if you can;   350
then later, when you are in need, he will be there.
                                    Make no evil profits;
evil profits are doom.[39] Be friendly with people friendly to you; visit
those who come visiting; give to those who give too, not to those who do not.
Anyone gives to a giver; a man who won't give won't get either.   355
For Give is a good thing, but Grab is an evil – she gives death.
When you give a gift willingly, even a large gift,
you will be glad in it; it will rejoice your heart as well,
but when a man grabs for himself, persuaded by shamelessness,
even only a small thing freezes his heart. For even a small thing,   360
when piled on a small thing, done often, grows large. Add to what you have
and keep off hunger.
                    Anything stored in the house
gives no grief. Things are better at home; something gone from the house   365
has harm standing by it. It is good to have things at hand
and a plague to want something gone missing – keep all that in mind.
       When you open a jar use it freely and don't spare at the end –
skimp in the middle; to spare at the dregs is just wretched.
       When you hire a friend agree on the wage; let it be sure.   370
If you hire your brother, smile; be pleasant – and see there's a witness;
trusting and mistrusting have both been known to destroy men.
       For women, don't let a tricked-out rear end fluster your mind.
Women wheedle and coax; all the time what they want is your barn.
Trust a woman – you might as well trust a thief.   375
                                    One son is best for the house;
he will nourish it and wealth will increase in the halls. If another is left,
dividing the property, plan to die an old man.[40] But still, Zeus

---

37   "Distinction" here translates the Greek word *timê*, "honor" or "prerogative," as in
       note 30 above. Here, however, it may simply mean "good value."

38   Although this line has been interpreted as referring to the need to defend oneself
       against a cattle raid, given Hesiod's generally unwarlike tendencies it is more likely
       that he has in mind the ubiquitous tendency of cattle to break out and wander off.
       The battle over the flocks of Oedipus (WD 163) belonged to an earlier time.

39   "Doom" here translates *atê*, as in note 24 above. I follow David Grene's translation
       in Nelson, 1998: "Make no ill profits; ill profits are just so much loss."

40   Literally "may you die old leaving behind another child". An alternate reading
       would give "may he [i.e. your child] die old leaving behind another child".

can provide riches even to more – more help is more care, and more
increase.   380
So for you, if your heart hopes for wealth, do this, and work and work
and work more.

[The Farmer's Year]

When Atlas' children, the Pleiades, rise, start your harvest;
plow when they set.[41] Forty nights and days they lie hid,   385
and then, as the year comes round, when the iron for mowing
is first sharpened, they appear.
This is the way of the plains,[42]
of those who live near the sea, and of those in the clefts
of the mountains, in rich land, away from the tossing sea: 390
strip to sow; strip to plow; strip to harvest,[43] if each in its season
you would care for the works of Demeter. So each in its season
will flourish – or else, afterwards, lacking, you may beg   395
at other men's households and gain nothing – as you have come now to me.
But I will give you no further measure. Work, Perses you fool,
work the works that the gods marked for men – lest someday you, children,
wife, and an ache in your soul, look for a living from neighbors
who don't care. Twice maybe, or three times, you may gain   400
your end; trouble them further and you will get nothing –
your fine speeches in vain, your words ranging useless. Instead, as I bid you,
think about undoing your debts and a way to shun hunger.
A house is the first thing, and a woman, and an ox for the plowing   405
– a woman you buy in, not one you marry, who can follow the oxen – [44]

---

41   The Pleiades, identified mythologically as the seven daughters of Atlas, rise (that
is, are visible just before sunrise) in the first half of May and set (no longer visible
at sunrise) in late October or early November. From the end of March to May they
are not visible at all, that is, they are "hidden." In a Mediterranean climate, in
which the winter is a season of rain and the summer of heat and drought, the land
is plowed and the crop sown in late fall to be harvested the following spring, after
the rains.

42   "Way" here translates *nomos*, as above, note 30.

43   The precept combines "works" and "days": one strips because effort is required
and because one should plow and sow early, while it is still warm.

44   Hesiod seems to have slyly amended a proverbial saying: "A house first, and a
wife, and an ox for the plow" by adding the next line. This is possible because the
Greek *gunê* means both "wife" and "woman." The Greeks used oxen for farm-work;
horses being considered a luxury of the rich (as *Prometheus Bound* 466).

and implements in the house, prepared and ready. Otherwise you may
ask another and he turn you down, and then you go lacking,
and the time in season pass by and the work is diminished. Don't put
things off   410
to tomorrow and then to the next day; no sluggish worker
fills up his barn, and neither does a man who delays.
It is care that prospers the work; Do-it-tomorrow wrestles with ruin.

[Autumn]

When the sun's strength leaves off its sweat and sharpness, in mid-autumn,   415
and strong Zeus sends rain and mortal complexions are eased
– for then the star Sirius travels little by day, over the heads of men
raised to destruction, and takes a greater share of the night,[45]
then the wood split with your iron ax is least worm-eaten, as the tree   420
pours its leaves to the ground and leaves off its sprouting.
Then be mindful of wood-cutting – for that is this season's work.
      A mortar takes three foot of wood, a pestle about four and a half;
for an axle you need seven foot – that is best suited – [46]
but if you cut eight, use what is left for a mallet. Cut a length   425
just over two feet for the wheel of a cart three feet long.
It is good to have many curved timbers: wood for a plow-tree,
whenever you find it, bring back to the house – look in the fields
for a holm-oak or else in the mountains; holm-oak is strongest
for plowing, when a wood-worker, Athena's servant, has fastened   430
the blade of the plow in with pegs and fitted it tight to the pole.[47]

---

45   Late September and early October.

46   Hesiod opens the farming section, which will, overall, be more descriptive than
informative, with detailed instruction designed to give it a businesslike air. Some
of the details may have become distorted in transmission as in the wheel for the
(literally two and a half foot) cart below. Here, for example, a seven-foot long axle
seems excessive, although West *WD* 264 reports wheel-ruts in Classical times from
wagons six feet wide.

47 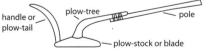 The pole connects the plow to the oxen
for pulling; the plow-tree connects
this to the plowstock or, (here) "blade"
which cuts the soil and which would
probably be fitted with an iron blade or "plowshare". The farmer holds the handle
or "plow-tail". As the plow-tree takes most of the strain Hesiod advises that it be
made of holm-oak, scarce in Boeotia, but very tough. Illustration taken from West
WD p. 266.

Keep two plows – toil on them at home – one naturally bent
and one joined together; it is best to have two. Then, if one breaks
throw the other on the backs of the oxen.
Laurel and elm   435
are least eaten by worms – they are best for the plow-pole;
use oak for the stock, holm-oak for the plow-tree, and get nine-year-old oxen,
two bulls, since their strength is unspent and their measure of youth
at its prime. These two are best at the work; they will not contend
in the furrow, breaking the plow, and leave the work there undone.   440
To follow them, a man in his forties is best, but a strong one.
Give him a decent sized loaf for his dinner, cut into eight slices.[48]
He will take care for the work and drive a straight furrow. Being past
looking around all the time for his friends, he will keep his mind
on the work. Another, no younger than him, is best to scatter the seed   445
and avoid over-sowing. A man more of a boy has his mind wandering
after his friends.
        When you hear overhead the voice of the crane, mark well
her clamor, high up out of the clouds; she brings the year's sign
for plowing and points out the season of winter and rain,[49]   450
and she gnaws at the heart of a man with no oxen. That is the time
to fodder your crooked-horned oxen inside in the barn.
For it is easy to say to a neighbor: "Give me your oxen and wagon,"
but the answer is easy too: "I have work for the oxen."
A man rich in daydreams sees a wagon already completed;   455
the fool forgets – a hundred planks are needed as well.
Take care for that first, and have them laid up in the house.
        But then when the plowing shows itself first to men who are mortal,
make haste, both you and your slaves, in both wet and dry, plowing   460
in the season of plowing, at the first light in the morning, hurrying
so that later your fields might be full. Plow land plowed first in springtime[50] –

---

48   Literally "a four-part, eight-piece loaf". Although the meaning is unclear the detail
      seems designed to produce a vivid image, hence my translation.

49   Late October and early November. See note 41 above for growing crops in a
      Mediterranean climate.

50   Literally "plow in spring; in summer plowing fallow [or, land lying fallow] will not
      deceive you". The elliptical expressions, like the jump below to prospects of the
      harvest, seem to follow the farmer's thoughts as he begins to plow, wonders if the
      land has been prepared well enough, and looks forward with pleasure or dread to
      the results of his labor. A field would normally be sown every other year and lie
      fallow in between, being broken with the plow as often as possible.

though fallow land broken in summer will not deceive you. Sow fallow
while the plowland is still light; fallow land defends against ruin; it quiets
the children.

    Pray to Zeus, god under the land, and to holy Demeter, that the grain 465
might be heavy, the grain of Demeter, and come to completeness.
Pray as you first start to plow, when the plow-handle is firm in your hand
and your stick comes down on the oxen, and they, with straps straining,
struggle to drag on the plow.[51] Let a small boy follow behind, a slave boy, 470
with a mattock, to cover the seed and make work for the birds.[52]
Have things arranged well; this for men is the best, as disorder is worst.
And so your grain-stalks will nod to the earth with their ripeness
if afterward the lord of Olympus himself gives good completion.
Then you may sweep the cobwebs from the grain bins, and, I think, then 475
you will be glad as you take from the livelihood stored up inside,
and in plenty you will come to grey spring, and not be looking to others
– but have another in need of you.
But, if you wait to plow
the good land until the sun turns at the solstice, you may sit down
to harvest, grasping thin handfuls of undergrown sheaves and, 480
dusty, bind them awry. So, not very pleased, you will bring home
a harvest that fits in a basket, and not many will be impressed.
But one way at one time, at another another is the mind of Zeus,
who bears the aegis;[53] it is hard for mortals to know. For if you
plow late, there could be this cure: when the cuckoo first cuckoos 485
from the oak trees, and men on the unbounded earth are made glad[54]

---

51   Literally "dragging the peg [that fastens the yoke on the oxen to the plow-pole] by
the strap". As above, Hesiod uses technical detail to render the picture vivid: the
peg would be the first thing the farmer would see taking up the strain as the plow
begins to move.

52   This line has been emended to read "let a slave follow a little behind", on the
grounds that the work is too hard for a child. Hesiod, however, does not tend to
be easy on his servants, and the image of a boy covering the seeds increases the
vividness. "Work" here translates *ponos*, otherwise translated as "toil."

53   The *aegis*, also commonly associated with Athena, is a goat-skin emblem made by
Hephaestus that terrifies enemies and can create thunderstorms. See *Theogony*
note 3.

54   The farmer who put off his plowing did not get to it until the winter solstice,
December 21st. The cuckoo arrives the following March, heralding spring. In
England, where the cuckoo arrives later, Shakespeare described King Richard as
like the cuckoo in June – heard but not regarded (*Henry IV.1* 3.2.75).

if Zeus should then rain on the third day and leave off
just when the tracks of the ox-hooves are filled but not overflowing –
then the late-plowing man may match one who plowed early.   490
Keep these things well in mind, all of them; don't let them escape you,
neither the time of grey spring nor the season of rain when it comes.

[Winter]

Pass right by the blacksmith's; keep away from its warmth and its chatter
in winter season, when the cold keeps a man from his fields; then a man   495
with no fear of work can do much to prosper his household.
Be careful of winter; it is a hard thing to deal with. It can catch you up
helpless and poor, using a thin hand to rub a foot that is swollen.
A man who won't work, with no livelihood, waits on a hope that is empty,
laying evils to heart. For no good hope keeps a poor man company   500
as he sits in the chatter-house[55] without any sure living.
        Tell your servants while it is mid-summer still:
"Summer won't last forever: now is the time to build sheds."

        But for the month of Lenaion[56] – avoid it; those days are evil;
they would take the skin off an ox, and the frosts that Boreas blows,   505
the North Wind, avoid them – they are cruel. He bellows
through horse-breeding Thrace and through the wide-ranging sea,
stirring it up with his blasts. The earth moans; the forest moans; in the valleys
the lofty-leaved oaks and thick pines, brought down, as he falls on them,
crash to the nourishing earth. Then the whole forest,   510
uncountable, roars. The beasts shudder, tucking their tails over their
privates, even those covered with fur. But for them too the cold
blowing goes through them, shaggy as they are. And it goes through
the hide of the ox – that cannot hold it back – and through the long hair   515
of the goat, but not the sheeps' fleeces; their wool is enough; the North Wind
does not blow through them, though it curves an old man like a wheel.
And through the soft skin of a girl the wind does not blow,
one who keeps in the house by her fond mother, not knowing yet   520
golden Aphrodite and her works; well bathed, her delicate skin
rich with rich oil, on a winter day she naps in a nook of the house,
while the squid, boneless one, gnaws his foot, deep in his fireless home   525

---

55   The Greek word Hesiod uses, *leschê*, could mean either lounge / hall or talk /
      chatter.

56   The second half of January and the beginning of February.

and pitiful haunts. The sun shows him no pasture to head for,
but goes instead to and fro over the cities and people
of men who are dark – and it sluggishly shines on all Greece.
    Then the beasts whose home is the woods, with horns and without,
take flight, wretched, their teeth chattering, through the thickets,   530
each with one care only at heart: it searches for shelter,
a thick-wooded corner, a rocky hollow to hide in.
Then, like an old man with bent back who sees only the ground,
his three legs barely enough – like him, wandering, they flee the white
snow.[57]   535

    Then wrap yourself up, and watch out for yourself as I bid you –
put on a soft cloak and clothes going down to your feet; make them .
of thick cloth, with more warp than woof; wrap them around you
to keep your skin calm, lest the cold raise the hair on your body.   540
Wear thick boots, close-fitting ones; make them from the hide of an ox
you have slaughtered. Line the insides with felt.
The skins of young goats, stitched together with ox-gut, thrown over your back,
keeps off the rain when the chill season comes. On your head wear a cap 545
of worked felt, to keep the wet from your ears – for dawn, in a north wind, is cold.
And at dawn, all over the earth, down from the sky of stars,
a wheat-growing mist spreads over the fields of the blessed,[58]
drawn from the ever-flowing rivers, raised by the gusts of the winds   550
high over the earth; at one time it rains down near evening,
at another blows on, when a Thracian north wind clusters the clouds.
Before it comes finish your work and go home. Don't let the dark cloud down
from the sky 555
wrapping round you, wet your skin, soaking your clothes. Avoid it,
for this month is the hardest, hard for flocks, with its winter and storms,
hard for men. Give the oxen just half their rations. For your man, though,
give him more – for the glad nights are long and can be great helpers.[59]   560
Keep this in mind until the year finds its end; balance the nights and days,
until earth once again, the mother of all, bears her commingled fruits.

---

57   As in the Sphinx's riddle (what goes on four legs in the morning, two in the
afternoon and three at night?) the "three-footed mortal" is an old man with his
stick.

58   "Fields" here is *erga*, also "works", as Introduction, p. 68.

59   The servant gets more than half-rations, but not full rations, since with the long
nights (great helpers) and little work to do one can sleep rather than eat. Since the
word "night" can be ill-omened Hesiod uses *euphronae*, "the glad ones" instead.

[Spring]

When sixty wintry days from the solstice, sun's turning, are done
and accomplished by Zeus, then Arcturus leaves Ocean' stream   565
to rise, shining out in the twilight.[60] After him comes the swallow,
Pandion's shrill-calling child, who appears when spring is beginning.
Before she comes, prune the vines; that is the best way to do it.   570
    But when the house-bearing snail climbs up the plants from the land
fleeing the Pleiades, then the time for digging the vineyard is over.[61]
Rather sharpen your sickle and stir up your slaves –
no sitting around in the shade and sleeping to dawn, when the time
for the harvest has come, the season the sun withers your skin.   575
Then be busy and gather your crops back to the house, rising early,
so your livelihood may be ensured. For dawn takes off a third
of man's work and dawn sends a man on his way,
and dawn sends on the work; dawn, who, in her shining   580
sets many a man on the road and puts many a yoke on the oxen.

[Summer]

But when the thistle flowers, when the cicadas sit in the trees,
shrill-chirping, and pour down in crowds their whistling whirring song
from under their wings, in the season of wearying heat,
then goats are the fattest, and wine the sweetest, and women   585
most randy – and men then are most feeble, when the star,
Sirius, parches their heads and their knees and skin dries up
in the heat.[62] Then is the time for cool shade by a rock,
for Biblos' wine, cakes made of milk, the milk of a goat drying-off,
and the meat of a heifer with no calf, grazed in the woods, and   591
of first-born kids. Then drink the bright wine, and sit in the shade,
with a heart glad of its dinner, a face turned to fresh-blowing Zephyrus.
Then you may pour from the springs always flowing   595
three measures of untroubled water, and the fourth a measure of wine.
    But for the slaves – hasten them on to Demeter's pure grain;
they need to get to the winnowing. Put them at it as soon as Orion

---

60   The second half of February.
61   Mid-May. The Pleiades have returned, as predicted in lines 383-4, to signal the
       harvest-time.
62   Mid-July.

appears.[63] Let the floor be well-rolled; make the place for the threshing
an airy one; then measure the grain and store it in jars – do it well.   600
And then, when the livelihood is put away in well-locked containers,
put your man out of doors.[64] A girl for a servant is best then –
one with no child; a worker with a calf under her is a trouble.
And attend to the watchdog; let him keep his teeth sharp
and don't spare his food, lest the man that does his sleeping in daytime
use some night to make off with your goods. Bring in fodder   605
and bedding for the oxen and mules, enough for the season – but then
let the men have a rest. There is time to relax; you can unyoke the oxen.
        But when Orion and Sirius move south, into mid-sky[65]
and rose-fingered Dawn sights Arcturus, then you, Perses,   610
cut off all the grape-clusters and carry them home. Show them the sun
for ten days and nights, then for five more shadow them over. The wine
will be ready to draw on the sixth. Put it in the jars; it is the gift
of glad Dionysus. And then when the strength of Orion, the Hyades,   615
and the Pleiades go below the horizon, remember – it is time for the plowing;
the season is here; may the full year lodge in fitness under the land.[66]

[Sailing]

                                                                But if longing
for sailing takes you, with its rough storms, then when the Pleiades
run from Orion's rude strength and plunge into the cloudy sea,   620
then all the winds rage; keep your ship well away from the wine-colored sea;

---

63   Orion first rose, for Hesiod, around June 20. He has switched the order of the
     summer picnic and the threshing, which would naturally follow the harvest, in
     order to create and then interrupt a sense of relaxation – there is always work to be
     done on the farm.

64   This line has also been taken as meaning "get a servant without a household" but
     after the harvest, when help is least needed, is a time for firing not hiring. The
     thes, or hired servant, is in some regards lower even than a slave, who at least has a
     household he belongs to. In the *Odyssey* (11.589-91) to be a *thes* to a poor farmer is
     the worst existence Achilles can imagine.

65   Mid-September. As above, note 41, Hesiod means when the stars are in mid-sky at
     dawn, that is, when the farmer emerges from his house and takes a first survey of
     the farm and the jobs for the day.

66   With the Pleiades' setting in October the year, and the description of the year, has
     come back to its starting point.

remember the land; as I tell you, work the earth.[67] For your ship,
haul it up onto shore and pack it round, on all sides, with stones
to hold off the winds' wet strength, and draw out the plug   625
to let out the bilge-water, so when Zeus rains the boat doesn't rot.
Get the rigging and the tackle all ready; store it away in the house.
Take down the sails, the boat's wings on the sea, and pack them up neatly,
and take off the rudder; hang it up over the fire to dry in the smoke.
And you, wait for the season for sailing; it will come soon enough –   630
then drag your ship to the sea; fill its swiftness with cargo,
and have the cargo well readied and fitted to win back gain for the house.
That was what your father and mine did, Perses, you fool – he used
to sail ships, stuck in the need for a livelihood. And then he came here,   635
crossing great stretches of sea in his black ship, leaving Aeolian Cyme behind,
not fleeing wealth or from an excess of riches or substance
but to escape need, evil poverty, that Zeus gives to men –
and he settled here, in a miserable village near Helicon,
Ascra, evil in winter, unpleasant in summer, never much good.   640
        But you, Perses, remember your work, all of your work,
in due season, but most of all about sailing.
A small boat is fine to praise, but your cargo should go in a big one,
for the greater the cargo, the greater the profit, and more upon that
in the future – if the winds hold back blasts of evil.   645
And if ever you turn to trade in your misguided heart, designing
escape from unlovely hunger and debt, I will point out
the measures of the much-sounding sea – not that I am much skilled
in sailing, since I never yet crossed the broad sea on a ship,   650
except once, when I went to Euboea from Aulis, where the Achaeans
lingered a long winter through[68] with a great host of the men
of holy Greece, gathered for Troy, land of fair women.[69]

---

67   November. This is also the time that Perses should be using for plowing, as in lines
      383-4. Despite his father's experience as a sailor (or, perhaps, because of it, 633-40),
      sailing for Hesiod seems to be purely an adjunct to farming, a way to gain a greater
      market for surplus goods, most likely olive oil and wine.

68   The distance from Euboea to Aulis, according to West, is about 65 meters of water
      – hardly an epic voyage. The Greek for "a long winter" could also mean "a long
      storm". Like Homer, who has no general word for "Greek," Hesiod uses "Achaean"
      to denote the Greek forces under Agamemnon.

69   Hesiod's epithets reverse the usual Homeric descriptions: "holy Troy" and "Hellas,
      land of fair women" (for Homer a region of Greece). In general Hesiod uses the
      regular epic descriptions ("formula"), as the "wine-dark" sea or "many-pegged"
      ships (660), but with a distinct lack of enthusiasm for sailing.

From there I crossed over too, for the games of war-minded[70]
Amphidamas, over to Chalcis. Many prizes were promised beforehand   655
by the sons of the great-hearted hero – and one, I may boast,
was mine, for my victory in song, a tripod with elegant handles.
That prize went to the Muses of Helicon. It was my offering,
where the goddesses set me first on the way to clear song.[71]
That is all my experience of many pegged-ships, but even so   660
I can speak Zeus' mind, for the Muses taught me unutterable hymn.[72]
       For fifty days after the solstice when the sun is done turning,
and the season's wearying heat has come to an end, then sailing
comes seasonable for mortals.[73] Then you are less likely to shatter   665
the ship and the sea drown the sailors – except when Poseidon,
land-shaker, or Zeus, king of immortals, is set on destruction –
for in them is the end of all, good and evil alike.
                                        At that time
the winds are set in good order; the sea is without harm.   670
Be of good cheer then; trust the winds; drag your ship to the sea
and load in the cargo; but hurry, and come home again quick as you can.
Don't wait for the new vintage of wine – and the strong rain in autumn
and the storms that come with it and fierce blasts of Notus, the south wind,   675
who stirs up the sea, keeping company with Zeus' strong storms,
the great rains of autumn, and makes the sea a harsh place for a sailor.
       There is another time for men to go sailing – in spring,
just at first, when a man sees the leaves on the fig tree, on the
very top branches, about the size of the track a crow makes   680
when she lights in her passing.[74] Then you can embark on the sea.
This spring sailing time – I don't like it; I wouldn't praise it;

---

70   Plutarch says that Amphidamas was killed during the Lelantine War between
     Chalcis and Eretria, which would date the contest to 730-700 B.C.

71   As described at *Theogony* 22-34.

72   "Unutterable," *athesphatos*, means, literally, beyond a god's uttering, hence both
     portentous and immense or immeasurable. Homer uses the word of vast entities,
     such as a storm, night, or the sea.

73   From the end of June through to August.

74   At the end of April. Just as the summer sailing fit in between the threshing and
     the vintage (producing the new wine one might bring back in trade, but that it is
     dangerous to wait for, 674) the spring sailing fits, just, between the time for pruning
     the vines and the harvest (564-73), a sign for Hesiod that Zeus (not necessarily out
     of the goodness of his heart) has set this as a time to sail.

it brings no joy to my heart. It is something men grab[75] – you
will hardly escape from disaster. And yet humankind, in its folly,   685
will do even this, since possessions, for wretched mortals, are life.

It is a terror to die in the waves; think about this, I bid you;
as I speak it out. Don't load all your livelihood into the hollow ships;
leave most behind; the smaller part take as your cargo.   690
For it is a terror to find misfortune at sea, in the waves,
and terrible if, when loading your wagon, the load overstrains it
and smashes the axle and the goods are all ruined.
Take care; keep watch on right measure; in all things fitness is best.[76]

[Marriage, Friendship, Society]

Bring a wife to your house in good season – when your age   695
is not much short of thirty, nor much over – marriage is seasonable then.
Your wife should be four years past girlhood; marry her in her fifth year
as a woman. She should be young so you can teach her customs and care.[77]
Most of all, marry someone who lives near. Look well about you   700
in this, for fear your marriage become a treat for the neighbors.
The best thing a man can seize is a wife – if she's a good one;
a bad one will freeze you. A wife who wants only dinners
burns a man up, even a strong man, without fire, and gives him
to an unripe old age.   705
Watch well for the wrath of the gods,
the blessed immortals. Do not make your comrade the same
as a brother. If you do, don't wrong him; don't be first doing evil.
Don't tell lies just to talk. But if he wrongs you first, with a word
that vexes, or a deed, remember, and pay him back double.   710
Then, if he is brought back into friendship, and will make amends,[78]
take it. A man who makes now this one his friend and now that one,

---

75   As with ill-gotten wealth (lines 320, 356) the need to "grab" is a bad sign for
      Hesiod. "Disaster" in the next line is literally "evil."

76   "Fitness" here is *kairos*, which came to mean primarily the right moment or the
      critical time for something.

77   A *parthenikê* or *parthenos* is an unmarried woman, and at four or five years
      past puberty (her "girlhood") she would be 18 or 19. As she is unmarried she is
      assumed to be a virgin, as Athena Parthenos is "Athena the Maiden" or "Athena the
      Virgin".

78   Literally: "he is willing to provide *dikê* ('justice')". Hesiod's relation to Perses
      seems to be hinted at here as also above: "With a brother smile, and get a witness"
      (371).

is worthless; looks and thoughts should keep company – see that yours do.[79]
    Don't be called every man's friend; don't be called no one's.   715
Don't get a name for having bad friends or for picking quarrels
with good people. And never taunt a poor man – don't dare;
poverty eats up the heart; it destroys a man, and it is given
by those blessed forever.
                A sparing tongue is a treasure
among men; to speak in measure the greatest grace. Those who speak evil 720
very quickly hear evil, and more evil, of themselves. Do it
and you will find out.
              And do not be rude at a pot-luck –
it's held for many; the pleasure and grace are the greatest,
and the cost least.

[Observances and Prohibitions]

           When at dawn you pour the flashing-eyed wine to Zeus,
don't do it with unwashed hands – or for the other immortals;   725
they will not hear you; they will spit back your prayers.
    Do not stand turned to the sun to make water. When he has set
and up to the time when he rises – remember – do not piss in the road,
nor just off the road as you walk. And do not uncover yourself;
the blessed gods are the keepers of night. A man who is godly,   730
who understands what is prudent, crouches or stands by the wall
of the well-fenced courtyard.
              After sex, when your privates are wet,
don't stand exposed by the hearth – avoid this. And don't beget generations
when home from a burial – that is ill-omened – but after a feast of the gods. 735
    Never, in the mouths of the rivers that flow out to the sea,
nor in the springs, make your water – and never relieve yourself.   758
Take care to avoid this, for it is far better so.[80]   759
    Don't cross a river's fair-flowing, ever-running water on foot
without prayer; look at the river's fair stream, and first wash your hands

---

79   Literally: "Do not let your mind (*noos*) convict your appearance of falsehood (*katelenchô*)".

80   These lines, 757-9, have seemed to a number of editors better suited here than closing the section, after the warning against mocking a sacrifice.

in the water, well-loved and clear.[81] The gods' nemesis follows
a man unwashed in hands and in evil, later they give him sorrow.   740
    Do not, at the gods' abundant feast, trimming the dry from the green,
pare the nails of your five-branching fingers with bright iron.
Do not set the wine-ladle on the bowl when people are drinking
– a ruinous fate is set there.[82] When building a house don't leave it
                                                   unfinished   745
or rough – lest a crow make his seat there and screech.
    Take nothing from unblessed cauldrons, either to eat
or to wash with; there is requital set also on that.
Do not put a twelve-day old boy on anything fixed, like altars and tombs; 750
it is bad and could unman him – the same for a boy of twelve months.
Don't brighten your body with water used by a woman
– a man should not – for the requital is dire there, at least for a time.
And, if you happen upon sacred rites, do not cast blame   755
as the sacrifice burns – the gods' indignation lies also on this.   756
    Do these things, and avoid mortal talk, for talk can be fearful.   760
It is an evil, a light thing to lift up – very easy – but painful to carry,
and hard to be rid of. No talk dies when many people have voiced her;
she too is a kind of a god.[83]

[The Days]

                      Watch for the days that are Zeus';   765
keep their right portions; point them out to your household. The thirtieth
is best to look over the work and allot the provisions –
where a people who distinguish the truth conduct their affairs.
For these are the days of the wise-minded Zeus:
                        To begin, the first, fourth, 770
and seventh are all holy days, the seventh most, since then
Leto bore gold-bladed Apollo – also the eighth and ninth. Two days
when the month is increasing are best for the toil of men's work –

---

81   In Greece, as elsewhere, many people now cross themselves before traveling across
    water. The word translated "sorrow" below, *algea*, is elsewhere "pain."

82   The bowl (*krater*) is used for mixing the wine with water, as was usual among the
    Greeks, the ladle for pouring it into cups.

83   Literally "avoid the fearful (*deinê* as also *WD* 687, 690, 691, where I translate
    as "terror" and "terrible") talk of mortals." Other manuscripts read "avoid the
    wretched (*deilê*) talk of mortals." Any entity that has a power beyond human
    control has, for Hesiod some element of the divine in it.

the eleventh and twelfth.[84] Both are good, either to shear or to reap   775
the glad crops – but the twelfth is better, since then, in the full of the day,
the air-swinging spider weaves and the ant, the wise one, reaps his store.
On that day a woman should set up her loom; it will forward the work.
  The thirteenth, in the first of the month, is a bad day   780
for starting to sow, but best for bedding in plants. The sixth
of the mid-month suits plants least, but for boys is a good day
to be born. For girls it is bad, a bad day to be born, a bad day to marry.
The first sixth is bad too for a girl's birth. On that day geld goats or sheep 785
or fence in a place for your flocks – the day smiles kindly on that.
And it is good for a boy's birth, a boy with a fondness for lies,
guileful words, taunts, and hidden whispers.
                              On the eighth geld a boar   790
or a strong-bellowing ox; mules, hard-workers, geld on the twelfth.
  The twentieth, a mighty day, at high afternoon, gives birth
to a wise man, one whose thoughts will be strong and close-packed.
The tenth is good for a boy to be born, the fourth for a girl
– in-mid month. On that day too gentle to the touch of the hand the sheep 795
and the shambling, crooked-horned cattle and a sharp-toothed dog
and hard-laboring mules. But take care on the fourth, at the month's waning
and its waxing – avoid the pain that eats out a man's spirit;
the fourth is a fateful day.
                        Bring a wife home on the fourth,   800
when you have looked at the omens, the ones that are best for the job.
  All fifth days are bad; avoid them; they are hard days and dire.
They say on the fifth Oath was born, with the Furies attending,
and Strife was the mother, and she bore him, the perjurer's plague.
  In mid-month, on the seventh, throw Demeter's pure grain   805
onto the threshing floor, but have a good look at it first,
and have the wood-smith cut wood for a bedroom, and for a ship,
plenty of it – the sort of thing suited to ships – but wait to the fourth
to put together the ship's narrow hull.

---

84   Hesiod calculates days from the first to the thirtieth, as we do, but also in three
     groups of ten, the waxing or increasing, the middle, and the waning or decreasing
     (originally following the waxing and waning moon), so that the third day of the
     middle month, for example, would be the 13th and the third of the waning month
     the 23rd.

                         The ninth of the mid-month   810
is better towards evening; the first ninth has no harm at all;
it is an excellent day, good to plant, good to be born in –
both for a man and a woman; it is never just bad.
The twenty-seventh – few know this – is the best day
to open a storage-jar. Yoke the necks of the oxen or mules then,   815
or the swift-footed horses. And on the thrice-nine haul a swift ship,
many-benched, down to the wine-colored sea. Few name this day truly.[85]
     Open a jar on the fourth. Above all, the fourth of the mid-month
is holy. Also, the day after the twentieth not many know –   820
it is best just as dawn breaks; towards evening the day is less good.

     These days bring succor to earth-dwelling men. The others
fall here and there, unfraught; they bring nothing. One man praises one,
another another – few know for sure. Sometimes those days are
a stepmother, sometimes a mother. A man flourishes in them and prospers 825
when, with these things in mind, he works, blameless to the immortals,
judging the birds' omens, and keeping away from transgression.

---

85   West takes the true name to be the one Hesiod uses, the "thrice-nine" day,
       presumable as opposed to the "twenty-seventh" or the "seventh of the waning
       month."

Appendix

The Psychology of the Succession Myth
An Essay by Richard Caldwell

This interpretation of the *Theogony* depends on two basic assumptions. The first is that all human beings have, and use, a mode of thinking which is inaccessible to ordinary consciousness. This hidden world of thought is nothing mystical; it is the ideas and fantasies, typically originating in the childhood experiences which form our personalities and often connected in some way with our adult life, which are kept in a state of permanent repression (that is, kept out of consciousness by an internal censoring process).

The second assumption is that myths, like dreams, express these unconscious ideas in a more or less disguised, or symbolic, form. Dreams seem to have two positive functions: to protect sleep by incorporating potential disturbances (such as hunger, noise, etc.) into a dream, and to protect mental stability by relaxing repression temporarily and allowing repressed ideas to enter dream-consciousness in some form. Recent studies of the physiology of dreaming, at any rate, have shown that people who are deprived of dreams (but not of sleep) within a few days begin to hallucinate, become depressed and anxious, and exhibit quasi-psychotic personality traits.

Myths, of course, have many functions: they can entertain, they can instruct, they can remember, they can justify, and so on. But there are two functions, related to one another, which seem to be operative in nearly all myths: to satisfy curiosity, and (like dreams) to express unconscious fantasies.

It might be objected at this point that the satisfaction of curiosity could hardly be a primary motive of myths, since it is essential that myths be repeated over and over, whereas curiosity would presumably be exhausted after the first telling. To answer this objection, we need only recall the universal demand of small children that their favorite stories be told again and again, their insistence that they be repeated faithfully and accurately (and also the mixture of joy and exasperation with which they greet any deviation). It may be that a compulsion to repeat is present here; that is, the pleasure of curiosity's initial satisfaction is so great that the experience can be repeated many times. But it is probably better to assume that the satisfaction (and re-satisfaction) of curiosity is combined with another function related to the child's emotional needs. In other words, there are two simultaneous satisfactions, one intellectual and the other emotional, which work together; the first achieves its purpose by answering questions, and the second in a number of ways (mastering fear, resolving emotional ambivalence, identification with a relevant character, etc.). When the evil stepmother disappears and the fairy godmother returns in the nick of time, the child learns two things: on an intellectual level, he learns how the story ends; on an emotional level, he realizes that the bad mother (who is in reality the punishing, disappointing, denying, or merely absent mother) is only a temporary presence, and that the real mother is the good mother who will surely return.

Myths also satisfy curiosity of many different kinds, although the underlying question is always "What was it like in the past?" In the case of a theogony, the object of curiosity is how the world began, how things started, how the world and its gods came to be the way it is believed they are. But this intellectual function is inseparable from an emotional goal, just as the child's question "Where do babies come from?" is really an expression of his concern over the details of his own conception, birth, and status.

The symbolic expression of unconscious needs energizes the other functions of myth. It is what makes myths moving and compelling, even for someone who no longer believes in their literal truth, and (just as in dreams) it attaches emotional energy to a varied, often seemingly unconnected, collection of memories. The most important difference, although not the only one, between myths and dreams is that dreams express the wishes and fears of a single individual, and these may be so personal and idiosyncratic, so tied up in an individual history, that they may be irrelevant or nonexistent for others. Myths, however, whatever their hypothetical beginning may have been, retain their status as myth only if the wishes and fears they express pertain to many or all of a population.

We should begin our study of the *Theogony* by returning to the issue of curiosity. To be curious about all sorts of matters is natural and appropriate for children; it is how they learn and grow, and its gradual loss is one of the unfortunate disasters of maturation. Among all the objects of childhood curiosity, however, there are two matters of special importance for dreams and myths, because they are intimately connected with the child's feelings and are most likely to produce anxiety and subsequent repression: the origin of the baby, and the difference between the sexes.

It is not difficult to see that these questions are really about the child's own birth and status, and about parental sexuality. The question "Where do babies come from?" is really a generalized expression of two questions of great emotional significance to the child: "Where did I come from?" and "How did my parents produce me?".

We might expect to find symbolic representations of these questions and their answers, and of the fantasies and memories associated with them, occurring frequently in myth. Every birth of a hero, for example, reflects to some extent the individual's repressed curiosity and ideas about the circumstances of his own birth. But it is especially in myths of the beginning of the world that we might anticipate finding a mythical version of the beginning of the individual.

The world, according to Hesiod, begins with the spontaneous emergence of four uncaused entities (116-120): Chasm (Chaos), Earth (Gaia), Tartarus, and Eros. Why these four, and why in this order? Chaos signifies in Greek a void or abyss, a vast and impenetrable darkness (see on 116). This totally undifferentiated state is followed by the appearance of Earth, from both an anthropomorphic and a psychological viewpoint, the cosmic projection of the mother.

If we regard the account of the world's beginning as a mythical representation of unconscious memories pertaining to the beginning of individual life, we may suppose that Chasm must symbolize a stage of life before any perception of the mother exists. There is in fact such a stage, which lasts for approximately the first six months of a child's life, and it is generally referred to in psychoanalytic language as the "symbiotic" state. The leading characteristic of this state is the child's inability to perceive the difference between itself and its environment; I and not-I, child and mother, self and world, are not differentiated from one another in a clear or stable way.

Around the middle of the first year of post-natal existence, this state comes to an end and the child becomes an individual, able to discern the difference between self and others; the new stage is called "separation-individuation." Although this transition is a gradual process rather than a sudden event, the key factor on which self-recognition depends seems to be a prior perception of the mother (or whoever functions as the mother) as separate. Only when the child realizes that the mother is a separate person (whose return, whenever she leaves the child, is thus always a question and a source of anxiety) is he able to view himself, as if in a mirror, as a separate individual.

The beginning of individuation is therefore the occasion for emergence of a self-identity, a rudimentary "ego"; but it is also the time when anxiety, frustration, and desire are experienced for the first time. During symbiosis pain and discomfort, as well as pleasure and gratification, are felt by the child, but they are not experienced as dependent upon something or someone external to the child. The newborn infant does not cry because he is left alone, nor does he even know that he is alone. The individuated child, however, perceives that most of his needs and wishes (which are few but urgent) depend for their fulfillment on a separate entity, the mother. It is only when the child is able to recognize that something is absent or lacking that frustration can occur, and the desire to have something depends on the prior recognition of not having it.

Although the symbiotic state is left forever, unconscious memories remain of a situation in which there can be no desire, since nothing is perceived as missing or separate from the all-inclusive symbiotic "self." These memories appear most obviously, in the myths of Greece and of virtually all cultures, as stories of a primal paradise at the beginning of the human race, a situation in which the first humans lead a life of total comfort and ease without pain, labor, or desire. The Garden of Eden in Genesis is the most familiar example of this paradisal fantasy, but there are parallels everywhere, including several in Greek myth; the closest is Hesiod's myth of the Golden Age, in which the first men are portrayed as living in happiness and abundance, "free of troubles and misery" and effortlessly possessing "all good things" (WD 109-120).

The symbiotic Golden Age appears only in the *Works and Days*, however, while the *Theogony* portrays symbiosis under another aspect: as an undifferentiated state prior to the emergence of the mother as the first object of the child's perception. The mythical name of this formless state is Chasm and the end of this state, in myth as in life, is brought about by the fact that what was once part of the self is now a separate object, the mother or Earth.

At this point in the mythical drama, symbiosis has ended and individuation has begun. The new individual experiences for the first time frustration and, as a result, desire for what is not present—for the mother, for gratification, and ultimately (and unconsciously) for restoration of the lost symbiotic state. This experience of primal lack and the beginning of desire, based on the perception of the mother as separate, occurs in Hesiod's myth as the appearance of Tartarus and Eros immediately after Earth.

In the *Theogony* Tartarus is both the underworld in general and the lowest place in the underworld (720-721), and it is a place of punishment. The Titans and the monster Typhon are put there after their defeat by Zeus (729-730, 868), and it seems to be the place where Sky (Ouranos) confines his children (see on 119). In subsequent Greek literature, Tartarus was gradually identified as that part of the underworld in which certain famous sinners suffered specific punishments. Although the list eventually became rather full, the four earliest and best-known sufferers in Tartarus are Tityus, Sisyphus, Tantalus, and Ixion. Their punishments all signify frustration, not only in the general sense of being confined and restrained but also in the specific details of each case. Tityus is tied down while two vultures eat his liver, which grows back monthly only to be eaten again; Sisyphus rolls a huge stone uphill, whereupon it rolls back down on him; Tantalus is perpetually hungry and thirsty, standing amid fruit and water which always elude his grasp; Ixion is fastened to a fiery wheel which perpetually revolves.

The crimes of these four, like their punishments, are also variations on the same theme. Tityus and Ixion each tried to rape one of Zeus' wives (Leto in the case of the former and Hera in the latter). Sisyphus saw Zeus' rape of Aegina and told her father Asopus. Tantalus' crime appears in three variants: he revealed the gods' secrets, or he stole ambrosia, or he killed his son Pelops, cooked him, and fed him to the gods. We will return shortly to the psychological meaning of these crimes.

Tartarus is therefore a place not only of punishment, but also of eternal frustration and loss. In the *Theogony* as well as in later accounts it is where the losers in generational conflict and unsuccessful usurpers are confined. But in its first appearance, immediately after Earth, Tartarus is a cosmic principle which represents the first crucial loss in the life of every individual—the irreversible loss of the symbiotic state and of the mother who has come to represent the earlier state of bliss.

This loss is the cause and condition of the first emergence of desire, which appears in the Hesiodic myth as Eros, fourth and last of the spontaneous primal beings. Hesiod's Eros is virtually an abstraction, a procreative principle in life and the cosmos; after Eros comes into existence, desire will be the controlling force in the development of the universe. But the immediate cause of the appearance of Eros is the prior existence of Tartarus. Frustration, the perception that something is lacking, is the necessary antecedent of desire, as Socrates says in the *Symposium* (200e): "Eros is always the desire of something, and that something is what is lacking." Or, in Hesiod's mythic terminology, Tartarus must come before Eros.

The first great loss for every individual is the loss of symbiosis, and the first desire is the impossible wish to recover that state. The cycle of lack and desire will continue in innumerable forms throughout life, once the individual has recognized that the absent objects which will fulfill desire are located outside himself and his control. But the next time that we find the combination of impossible desire and inevitable loss occurs at the time of the Oedipus complex, the climactic episode of childhood psychological development. The Oedipus complex may be defined most generally as the child's possessive and jealous wishes concerning the parent of the opposite sex and related feelings of rivalry and hostility toward the parent of the same sex. In the case of the male child (the usual reference in Greek myth), this involves the son's desire to replace his father in the attention and affection of his mother, and his fantasies both of removing the father and of gratifying the mother in whatever way she requires (and in whatever way the child imagines that the father performs this task).

The Oedipus complex is of course the basic principle of the *Theogony*'s narrative plot, a cycle of generational conflict in which mothers favor their sons and sons overcome their fathers, until Zeus finally puts an end to the repetitive pattern. But the Oedipus complex is also a critical re-statement of the inevitable loss and impossible desire which characterize the end of symbiosis in particular and the situation of individuated life in general.

This reciprocity appears in Hesiod's portrayal of Tartarus as both a primal being and as a prison for oedipal criminals. The situation of the Titans is somewhat different from that of the four criminals later placed in Tartarus, since the Titans are at least partially successful in their oedipal endeavor. Sky also had succeeded in part, marrying his mother but not overthrowing his father (he doesn't have one), and the Titans overthrow their father but do not marry their mother. It is, in fact, only after the appearance of Zeus that the impossibility of oedipal desire is established. He cannot be overthrown, and since removal of the father is a prerequisite to possession of the mother, the oedipal project is henceforth doomed to failure.

The two key instances in the *Theogony* of an unsuccessful oedipal rebellion against Zeus are his conflicts with the monster Typhon and the Titan Prometheus. Neither of these potential usurpers is actually a son of Zeus, but, as we shall see, both of them are substitutes for an identifiable son. In particular, the struggle between Zeus and Prometheus in the central panel of the *Theogony* is clearly related to the situation of the oedipal criminals in Tartarus; his punishment is almost exactly the same as that of Tityus, and his crimes are similar to those of Tantalus. Prometheus steals the gods' fire and Tantalus steals their ambrosia, and both of them attempt to deceive the gods at a banquet.

At this point it may be helpful to look more closely at the crimes of the four inhabitants of Tartarus. If we assume that the gods are psychological representations of the parents, and in particular that Zeus represents the father, the meaning and similarity of these crimes is apparent. Ixion and Tityus are the most straightforwardly oedipal, since each of them attempts to rape one of Zeus' wives. The crime of Sisyphus, that he spied on Zeus' sexual activity and then revealed the "secret," is also oedipal, a fulfillment of the child's wish to see a forbidden sexual sight and to learn the secrets of parental sexuality.

Tantalus, like Sisyphus, is said to have revealed the "secrets" of the gods, and the oedipal nature of this crime appears also in his other two crimes: 1) he stole ambrosia, and 2) he was so obsessed with proving himself superior to the gods that he cut up and served his son Pelops to the gods for dinner, figuring that if any of the gods ate a piece of Pelops, this would prove that he knew something they did not know (Pindar, *Olympian* 1). The cannibalistic banquet is both oedipal and "counter-oedipal": at the same time that he attempts to prove himself superior to Zeus (who is his real, as well as symbolic, father), Tantalus tries to eliminate the potential threat of his own son (just as Sky and Cronus tried to do).

Tantalus' theft of ambrosia, like the theft of fire by Prometheus, is the metaphoric expression of an oedipal desire not only because each substance is a jealously guarded divine (i.e., paternal) prerogative, but also because both ambrosia and fire have demonstrable sexual meanings. Ambrosia is relatively unimportant in Greek myth, but its symbolic meaning can be seen by comparing it to its linguistic and mythical equivalent in Hindu myth, the divine food called amrta in Sanskrit. Both ambrosia and amrta literally mean "immortality," and that is what consumption of these foods confers on the Greek and Hindu gods. But, in addition, amrta and soma (the other and more common Sanskrit word for ambrosia) are explicitly associated in Hindu myth with semen and paternal sexuality. There are numerous Hindu myths of the theft of amrta or soma from the gods, which are similar to (and often combined with) stories of the theft of fire (which also symbolizes paternal sexuality). Greek and Hindu myths are both Indo-European, and there would seem to be a vast and pervasive Indo-European complex of myths in which the theft of fire or the food of immortality represents an oedipal assault on the paternal privileges of the sky-god.

Even if we did not know about the Hindu parallels and other Indo-European material, however, there is ample evidence in Greek myth that the thefts of fire and ambrosia are symbolic equivalents, and that both represent an attempt to take for oneself the sexual position of the father-god. Although Prometheus is not punished in Tartarus as is Tantalus, the nature of the punishment he receives is almost exactly the same as that of Tityus, who is in Tartarus; both are confined while a bird or birds eat their livers, which are periodically renewed after being consumed. If the punishments of Prometheus and Tityus are the same, their crimes are presumably equivalent, and Tityus' attempted rape of Zeus' wife is an oedipal offense.

The same principle holds true for Tantalus, who is in Tartarus for stealing ambrosia. Since the crimes of the others who are there, as well as his own crimes in other versions, are overtly oedipal, the theft of ambrosia would also seem to be oedipal. Furthermore, ambrosia (in Tantalus' crime) and fire (in Prometheus' crime) are structurally equivalent, as we have seen, and fire (especially the fiery lightning-bolt) is associated with the sky-god's sexual power in Greek and other myths.

The first of the Greek sky-gods is Sky, whose marriage to his mother Earth establishes an oedipal precedent from the beginning. This union of Sky and Earth, creates an interesting problem: if they are to be the first parents, how do they join together to produce children? How can the sexual intercourse of Sky and Earth be represented? The obvious, and perhaps earliest, answer is that the rain which falls from the sky onto the earth is the semen of Sky. As Aeschylus says in a fragment of his tragedy *Danaides*, "Rain falling from Sky makes Earth pregnant." The same symbolism underlies the frequent occurrence in many origin myths of water and earth as the elements from which a creator-god makes the first humans, as in Hesiod's account of the creation of Pandora by Hephaestus (WD 60-61). In some instances this creative clay is made from earth and spit, and the sexual symbolism is more explicit; the water which impregnates earth is a bodily fluid (the same symbolism appears in the English saying that someone is the "spit and image of his father"). The most obvious sexual allusion, however, appears in the word *ouranos* itself, a noun related to the verb *ourein* ("to urinate"). Sky (Ouranos), he-who-rains, is in fact "he-who-urinates."

The other means by which the sky comes into contact with the earth, and therefore the other cosmic symbol for the sky-god's sexual power, is lightning. This significance not only appears in references by Greek philosophers to fire as the generative element in nature, but also plays a role in the myth of Zeus' affair with Semele, a mortal princess of Thebes. Tricked by Hera into insisting that Zeus have sex with her in the same way that he did with his divine wife, Semele was incinerated by the lightning of Zeus, who burst through the bedroom door driving a chariot and hurling thunderbolts. The sexual power of Zeus is a force so powerful that no mortal woman can tolerate its full expression, and its symbol is the fire of Zeus' lightning.

The elemental opposites fire and water, lightning and rain, are thus the cosmic projections of the sky-god's paternal sexuality, and the theft of fire by Prometheus is an oedipal attack on Zeus. The first oedipal revolt in the *Theogony*, however, occurs in the first generation of the gods. Sky, married to his own mother, tries to prevent his sons from overthrowing him and taking away his privileges. Earth and her sons then conspire together to defeat Sky, who is castrated by Cronus, the younger generation becomes the older, and the sons become the new fathers. But if this is true, why do the Titans not try to marry their mother Earth, just as Sky had married his? Although the ultimate goal of the Oedipus complex is presumably the fulfillment of the son's wish to become the sexual partner of his mother, there is no indication that the Titans want or attempt to marry their mother. Four of the Titans sons marry their sisters (Ocean marries Tethys, Hyperion Theia, Coeus Phoebe, and Cronus Rhea),

Crius marries his half-sister Eurybia, and Iapetus marries his niece Clymene. Earth does in fact marry another of her sons after the downfall of Sky, but her new husband is not one of the Titans; he is her youngest parthenogenic son Sea (Pontus), by whom she gives birth to three sons and two daughters (233-239).

An answer to this problem, which will be repeated in the case of Zeus, is that the succession myth presents a kind of progression in which each generation tries to get what it wants without repeating the mistakes of the previous generation. Thus the Titans deposed their father and won his sexual power but then, not wanting to suffer the same fate as he had incurred, they chose to exercise their new sexual freedom by marrying their sisters or other relatives but not their mother.

Nevertheless, the sexual nature of the conflict between the Titans and their father is made clear by its outcome in the fact of castration. Furthermore, Earth is not entirely absent from the sexual objective of her son Cronus, who replaces his father as lord of the sky and marries Rhea, his sister but also an earth-goddess like her mother. The same thing will happen in the next generation when Zeus, the third sky-god, marries the earth-goddesses Right (Themis) and Demeter.

As we have seen, the steps Cronus takes to protect his position are clearly derived from his memory of what had happened to his father and from his intention that nothing similar happen to himself. The lesson Cronus learns from the fate of Sky is basically misogynistic; he sees that it is the woman as much as the son who is his enemy. His children must not be allowed an independent existence, and they must be kept away from their mother, their potential accomplice. For these reasons Cronus decides to swallow each of his children as they are born, but his strategy fails and once again the sky-god is overthrown by his deceiving wife and ambitious son.

The filial agent of Cronus' defeat is his youngest son Zeus, and the fact that he is youngest is appropriate to his role as the successor of Cronus, just as Cronus was the youngest of the children of Sky. In myth it is typically the youngest son who inherits the father's position, and it is not difficult to see the psychological reason for this in the dynamics of sibling relationships. From the perspective of an older child, it is always the youngest who inherits, who displaces his predecessors in the affection and attention of his parents. In the Greek succession myth the conflict between the societal law of primogeniture (inheritance by the eldest) and the psychological law that the youngest child must usurp the privileged position of his older brothers is neatly solved by the imprisonment of the children as they are born in one or another parental body. When the Titans are released from the body of Earth or when the Olympians are disgorged from the body of Cronus (in each case, a kind of second birth), the order of birth is reversed. Cronus, the youngest of the Titans, is closest to the surface of Earth and thus the first to be (re)born, and Zeus, youngest of the children of Cronus, moves to the position of eldest by escaping being swallowed and subsequent rebirth. In this way youngest becomes eldest, and psychological reality is mythically verified.

The conflict between Sky and Cronus had ended in an actual castration, such a conclusion being not only psychologically appropriate but also literally necessary in order for the children to escape from their mother's body. Now, in the second generation, freedom and victory are not simultaneous, as in the first, but are separate events; the children are freed by the ruse of the same Earth who gave Cronus the sickle, and victory is later achieved by the superior power of Zeus and his allies. Although Cronus does not suffer a literal castration, he and his defeated fellow-Titans are imprisoned in Tartarus, a place of symbolic castration, and it should also be noted that the weapon which gives Zeus his military superiority is the lightning which represents his sexual preeminence.

Now that Zeus has become the new sky-god and lord of the universe, he faces two related tasks: he must find a way of avoiding the fate suffered by his father and grandfather, and he must then populate the world with the gods and heroes whose production will consume most of his time and energy from now on. The second task, which will establish the structure of Greek heroic myth, depends on completion of the first, since it is the security Zeus wins which gives him the opportunity of virtually unchecked procreation. The first task is also both climax and conclusion of the succession myth; by succeeding in it, Zeus will escape from the cycle of oedipal overthrow which conquered his predecessors.

The logically necessary solution discovered by Zeus (In 17-18) is to swallow his first wife Intelligence (Metis). Cronus had erred in thinking that he could succeed by separating his sons from their mother, but Zeus now realizes that the real enemy is his wife, and by swallowing Intelligence he prevents the birth of the son who is destined to overthrow him. This is only the first step in Zeus' strategy, however; he has a dual problem, wife and sons, and he will deal with each part of the problem separately. The seven wives of Zeus are, in order, the Oceanid nymph Intelligence, the Titanid Right, another Oceanid Eurynome, Zeus' sister Demeter, another Titanid Memory (Mnemosyne), the second-generation Titanid Leto, and finally his sister Hera; the relationships of the seven to Zeus are cousin-aunt-cousin-sister-aunt-cousin-sister. Once he has secured his reign by swallowing Intelligence, the first wife, it seems that all other possible relationships are now open to him.

There is, of course, one important exception: unlike Sky, who had married his mother Earth, and like Cronus and the Titans, who married their sisters but not their mother, Zeus stops short of mating with his mother Rhea. Nevertheless, just as Rhea had been virtually a mother-figure to her husband Cronus, Zeus now marries two of his mother's sisters (Right and Memory) and two earth-goddesses (Right and Demeter). But since marrying mother-substitutes instead of the actual mother had not saved Cronus from being overthrown, Zeus must do more than merely refrain from marrying Rhea herself.

Or, to put it another way, Cronus may be said to have married his mother under the guise of Rhea, her double, just as Sky had married his mother Earth. With Zeus it seems that the scenario will be repeated again, since both maternal figures, Earth and Rhea, contrive to save him from his father. But in Zeus' case there is an important difference: although he has a sexual relationship with two aunts and several maternal goddesses, he observes at least a rudimentary distinction between permissible and non-permissible sexual objects. His establishment of a primal incest taboo occurs in his first marriage; to avoid having the son who will overthrow him, Zeus must give up the woman who will be that son's mother.

Zeus then proceeds to atone for this act of restraint by copulating with practically every woman in Greek myth. There is, however, one other occasion on which he is forced to limit his sexual activity, a limitation perhaps required by the fact that he had not abstained entirely from a sexual relationship with Intelligence. In a myth appearing in several variants, Zeus is said to have learned that an unnamed woman was fated to bear a son who would be greater than his father. There could be no worse news for Zeus than this, since, if that woman exists somewhere in the world, she may be the next conquest in his procreation campaign. If he cannot discover her name, he must abandon sex or be overthrown. The one person who knows the identity of this woman is Prometheus, who has been sentenced by Zeus to eternal torture for his theft of fire, and he is not about to do an unrequited favor for Zeus. Once again Zeus has a simple choice and an inescapable decision: he must either give up sex entirely (which he cannot do), or he must free Prometheus in return for the name of the one woman he must renounce. He of course chooses the latter, and discovers that the woman is the Nereid nymph Thetis—who is, in one version, the current object of Zeus' amatory attention. Zeus forces Thetis to marry the mortal Peleus, a hero but not too much of one (having been defeated in wrestling by a woman, Atalanta), and their son is Achilles (1006-1007), a truly great hero but not the new sky-god.

Just as there are two occasions on which Zeus' strategy of observing at least a minimal restraint in regard to a current or potential wife is successful, the *Theogony* contains two exemplary instances in which he succeeds in overcoming an attempted oedipal rebellion. The success of his first strategy clearly does not imply that his position is free from attack, but rather that any oedipal assault on him will fail. Each of these two examples of unsuccessful rebellion occupies a prominent position in the *Theogony*; the first is the conflict of Zeus with Prometheus (521-616) and the second is his war with Typhon (820-868). The most obvious fact about both of Zeus' rivals is that neither of them is his son. Nevertheless both of them are closely connected with a god who may or may not be the son of Zeus and Hera, and who may be the oedipal rival underlying the myths of Prometheus and Typhon. This god is Hephaestus, the "Lame One," the god of metallurgy, fire, and magic.

In the *Odyssey* Hephaestus is the son of Zeus and Hera (8.312); in the *Iliad* the same parentage is assumed by most readers of 1.578 and 14.338, although the identification is somewhat ambiguous. In Hesiod's account (927-929), however, and in most post-Hesiodic versions he is the parthenogenic son of Hera alone. According to Hesiod, Hera produced the fatherless Hephaestus because she was angry with Zeus. Although the cause of her wrath is not mentioned by Hesiod, the preceding three verses (which interrupt the account of Zeus' marriage with Hera) tell how Zeus "himself bore from his head owl-eyed Athena," the daughter with whom Intelligence had been pregnant when Zeus swallowed her. It appears that the cause of the quarrel was Zeus' newfound ability to produce children by himself, a slight to which Hera responded with the parthenogenesis of Hephaestus.

The defeats of both Sky and Cronus began when their wives grew angry and took independent action as a result of their husbands' interference with the normal process of birth, and it certainly seems as though the scenario is about to be repeated in the third generation. But we hear no more about the matter from Hesiod, for whom Zeus is now and henceforth secure in his position as master of the universe, with all challenges past and overcome.

For a suggestion of conflict between Zeus on one side, and Hera and Hephaestus on the other, we must turn to the *Iliad*, which contains two contradictory versions of Hephaestus' relations with his parents. In *Iliad* 1.590-594, Hephaestus cautions his mother against continuing her quarrel with Zeus by reminding her that once before Zeus had ended a dispute by punishing her, and furthermore had thrown him out of the sky:

> At another time, when I tried to help you,
> he seized my foot and threw me from the gods' threshold.
> All day I fell, and with the setting sun
> I landed on Lemnos, and little life was still in me;
> after I fell, Sintian men rescued me.

In *Iliad* 18.395-398, however, Hephaestus contradicts his own earlier story and claims that he was thrown from the sky by Hera, who was ashamed of the lame child to whom she had given birth. In this version, Hephaestus falls not on the island of Lemnos but into the sea, where he is rescued by the goddesses Eurynome and Thetis:

> She [Thetis] saved me, when I suffered, falling far
> by the will of my dog-faced mother, who wanted to
> hide me since I was lame; then I would have suffered
> in spirit if Eurynome and Thetis had not received me.

The only thing these two versions have in common is Hephaestus' fall from the sky, while they differ in who threw him, when and why he was thrown, how he became lame, and who rescued him. And yet both versions could correspond with a hypothetical myth in which an angry Hera bore Hephaestus by herself in order to gain revenge on her husband. In the *Iliad* 18 version her plan is thwarted by the lameness of her parthenogenic son, whom she abandons when he does not live up to her expectations. In *Iliad* 1, however, Hephaestus seems to be playing the role of the oedipal rival on the recalled occasion when he fought against his father on behalf of his mother.

There may well have been a pre-Hesiodic theogonic variant in which Zeus had to defend his position and claim to permanent rule by overcoming a challenge brought by his own son. In this variant Zeus would have faced exactly the same sort of rebellion as those which undid his father and grandfather. Unlike them, he would have defeated his son and thrown him out of the sky (like Milton's Lucifer), and thus put an end to the cycle of oedipal succession.

While a remnant of this hypothetical myth may have survived in the *Iliad* 1 account of enmity between Zeus and Hephaestus, the Hesiodic tradition—perhaps Hesiod himself—chose to suppress it in favor of an alternate account of conflict between Zeus and a fire-god, the rebellion of Prometheus. There are many possible reasons why this displacement may have taken place, the most likely of which center on Hesiod's conception of the nature and role of Zeus (e.g., the desire to make Zeus' victory the result of wisdom rather than force), but the possibility that it took place is supported by a complex of evidence in the *Theogony* and other surviving Greek literature.

The connection between Hephaestus and Prometheus extends far beyond the underlying fact that they are both fire-gods; there are several other specific situations in which the two are closely related and sometimes functionally interchangeable. For example, there are versions in which Prometheus is called a son of Hera (scholia to *Iliad* 5.205, 14.295) and both Prometheus and Hephaestus are said to have fallen in love with Athena (scholia to Apollonius

Rhodius 2.1249; Apollodorus 3.14.6); both Hephaestus and Prometheus are said to have assisted at the birth of Athena from the head of Zeus (Euripides, *Ion* 455; Pindar, *Olympian* 7.35); Hephaestus created Pandora by mixing earth and water (*Th.* 571) and Prometheus was credited with the creation of mankind by the same means; both Hephaestus and Prometheus were honored as the bringers of culture and technical advancement to humanity (Aeschylus, *Prometheus Bound* 436-506; *Homeric Hymn to Hephaestus* 2-7); Hephaestus was called the father or grandfather of the Lemnian Cabeiroi, and Prometheus was named as one of the Theban Cabeiroi (Strabo 10.3.21; Pausanias 9.25.6); in Attica the shrines and cults of Hephaestus and Prometheus were closely associated.

Given this network of associations, it is not difficult to see how Prometheus could replace Hephaestus as the defeated rival of Zeus, especially since the crime of Prometheus, the theft of fire, is an oedipal offense. And yet the conflict between Zeus and Prometheus is essentially concerned with cleverness and deceit, in which Prometheus regularly has the upper hand until finally Zeus tires of the game and consigns Prometheus to his cliff and man-eating eagle. There is nothing of the cosmic violence which marked the struggles of previous generations and which is suggested in the *Iliad* 1 account of the confrontation between Zeus and Hephaestus. For this aspect of Zeus' victory, we must turn to another Hephaestus-substitute, the monster Typhon.

Hesiod calls Typhon the son of Earth and Tartarus, and does not mention any connection between the monster and Hera. In two other versions, however, Typhon is closely linked to Hera, her enmity with Zeus, and (either directly or indirectly) with Hephaestus. In one version (scholia to *Iliad* 2.783) Earth, angered by the death of the Giants, complained to Hera, who asked Cronus for help. He gave her two eggs smeared with his semen and told her to bury them in the ground, predicting that from them would be born an avenger who could overthrow Zeus. She buried the eggs in Cilicia and Typhon was born, but Hera then was reconciled with Zeus; she told him what had happened and he killed Typhon with a thunderbolt.

In the other version (*Homeric Hymn to Apollo* 305-356), Hera, angry because Zeus had produced Athena by himself whereas her own attempt at parthenogenesis had resulted in the crippled Hephaestus, whom she had thrown from the sky (as in *Iliad* 18), prayed to Earth, Sky, and the Titans that she would bear a son greater than Zeus. A year later she gave birth to Typhon and entrusted him to the serpent Pytho to raise:

> Once she [Pytho] received from gold-throned Hera and raised
> terrible and cruel Typhon, a plague to mortals.   306
> Hera bore him since she was angry with father Zeus,
> when he, Cronus' son, bore illustrious Athena

in his head; mistress Hera grew immediately angry
and spoke among the assembled immortals: 310
"Hear from me, all gods and goddesses,
how cloud-gatherer Zeus begins to dishonor me
unprovoked, after he made me his true and good wife.
Now without me he bore owl-eyed Athena,
who is eminent among all the blessed immortals.   315
But my son was born the weakest of all gods,
Hephaestus with crippled feet, whom I bore by myself.
I seized him and threw him into the wide sea.
But Nereus' daughter, silver-shod Thetis,
rescued and cared for him with her sisters;   320
she should have done some other favor for the blessed gods.
Bold and clever one, what else will you now plot?
How dared you bear owl-eyed Athena alone?
Would I not have borne a child? At least I am called
yours, among the immortals who possess the wide sky.   325
Take care I do not plot some future evil for you.
Even now I will arrange to give birth to a son,
who will be eminent among the immortal gods,
without disgracing the holy bed of you and me.
I will not come to your embrace, but going far   330
from you I will be with the immortal gods."
Saying this with angry heart she left the gods.
Then cow-eyed mistress Hera prayed at once,
struck the ground with flat hand, and said:
"Hear me now, Earth and vast Sky above   335
and Titan gods who live under the earth
in great Tartarus, ancestors of men and gods.
All of you now listen and give me a son apart from
Zeus and just as strong as Zeus; rather, may he be
stronger, as wide-seeing Zeus is stronger than Cronus."   340
Saying this, she struck the earth with her great hand;
and life-bearing Earth was moved; seeing this, she felt
joy in her heart, for she thought it would come to pass.
From then on until the year's completion
she never came to the bed of wise Zeus   345
nor to the carved chair, where formerly
she sat and planned dense counsels,
but she stayed in her crowded temples

and enjoyed her offerings, cow-eyed mistress Hera.
But when the months and days were fulfilled   350
and the seasons passed through the circling year,
she bore a child unlike gods or mortals,
terrible and cruel Typhon, a plague to mortals.
Quickly cow-eyed mistress Hera took and gave him
[to Pytho], one evil thing to another; and she received   355
him; and he did many wrongs to the famous races of men.

The most striking fact about this version is that Typhon is conceived by
Hera in the same way and for the same reason that Hephaestus is conceived in
Theogony 924-929. This version also gives us, in effect, the background of the
Iliad 18 account (i.e., why Hera bore the crippled Hephaestus) and both versions
provide the aftermath of the *Theogony* 927-929 account (i.e., what happened
to Hephaestus after his parthenogenic birth). Although the *Theogony* does not
mention Hera's ill-treatment of Hephaestus, and Homer in *Iliad* 18 does not
mention a quarrel between Zeus and Hera, the two accounts along with the
Hymn to Apollo seem unmistakably to represent a tradition in which Hera
gave birth to Hephaestus in order to avenge herself against Zeus and in which
Typhon and Hephaestus play similar roles.

If in fact these two major digressions in the *Theogony*, the episodes involving Prometheus and Typhon, are Hesiod's reworking of another version
in which Zeus' final victory was over his own son, we may conclude with a few
speculations concerning the motivation for this displacement.

Zeus, as Hesiod continually reminds us, is the ultimate paternal figure,
the "father of gods and men." But this ultimate father is also a good father, who
maintains his rule not by the defeat and punishment of his sons but by victory over a thief and a monster. He is totally unlike his father and grandfather,
whose relationship with their sons was pure hostility and violence and who
were implacably opposed to generation itself. Zeus, on the other hand, has the
intelligence and, in a sense, sufficient self-restraint to avoid a repetition of the
past.

Perhaps more importantly, the *Theogony* is concerned not so much with
the present (that is, the unchanging present of the gods once Zeus has won
dominion) as with the past and how things came to be as they are. It is in the
present that Zeus is Father, and Hesiod shows us the implicit but certain logic of
Zeus' ascent to permanent paternity and sovereignty. Underlying the logical in-
evitability of Zeus' triumph, however, is an emotional imperative of equal force,
whose focus is not Zeus as idealized Father in the present but Zeus as idealized
Son in the past. His triumph represents the replacement of fathers by their sons,

and even his paternal role (i.e., endless procreation) is the wish-fulfilling result of his oedipal victory. He wins the fulfillment of divine sons' dreams—virtually unlimited sexual access to goddesses and women—and, thanks to his strategic observance of a small but significant exception to this availability (his swallowing of Intelligence and avoidance of Thetis), no ambitious son will appear to challenge his rule and take his place. If Hephaestus once was such a son, Hesiod has erased this fact and replaced it with Zeus' victories over Prometheus and Typhon, both of whom are associated primarily with the Titans and the older generation.

Zeus, the hero of Hesiod's vision, is the all-conquering son, the supreme example of an oedipal success story. In this myth, whose primary intellectual function is the description and explanation of the origin of the world and its gods, the narrative is impelled and energized by an emotional structure of symbiotic memories, oedipal wishes, and filial ambitions.

The story of Pandora provides an interesting example of this intellectual and emotional interaction. At first glance it might seem that the only emotional motivation present in the episode is misogyny, a view of women as at best a necessary evil and a great plague (*Theogony*), or as responsible for the presence of evil and suffering in the world and the necessity of labor (*Works and Days*). But if mortal woman is to be true to the divine precedents of the *Theogony*, she must be a "lovely evil" (Th 585) to her husband, since this is the role assumed by the divine wives in the succession story. If sons overthrow their fathers, it is not only because that is the way things are but also, and specifically, because mothers favor their sons. If women appear as dangerous and evil in the story of Pandora, this is simply an extension of the roles of Earth and Rhea, whose maternal allegiances regularly turn them against their husbands. From the viewpoint of the son, the good mother is necessarily a bad wife, since she must take the side of her son against her husband. And the viewpoint of the son is the viewpoint of the *Theogony*.

Index

References are to pages in the text except: following Th when they refer to line numbers in the *Theogony*, following WD when they refer to lines in the *Works and Days*. A lowercase "n" indicates references to footnotes in the *Theogony* (Th) or *Works and Days* (WD).

Circe (daughter of Helios), Th 957, 1011; Th n104, n110

(Mt) Cithaeron, in Boeotia (*see also* mountains), 68; Th n14

city (*polis*), WD 527; and justice, WD 189, 221, 227, 240, 269; city-destroyer, Th 936

Clio (Glorifying, one of the Muses), Th 77

closeness, *see* fondness

Clotho (Spinner, one of the Fates), Th 218, 905; Th n95

Clymene (Oceanid nymph, wife of Iapetus), 107; Th 351, 508; Th n67

Clytia (one of the Oceanids), Th 352

Cnossus (city on Crete) 3; Th n102

Coeus (a Titan), 13, 16; Th 134, 404; Th n6

comrades (*hetairoi*), WD 183, 706-711

contend (*eris*), *see* strife

contests (*aethla*), *see* ordeals

Corinth (a city in Greece), Th n48, n70

Cottus (a Hundred-Handed), Th 149, 618, 654, 714, 734, 817

counsel / design (*boule*), Th 121; to take counsel, WD 266, 647
Zeus and Prometheus, Th 534, 572
of Zeus, Th 465, 653, 667, 730; WD 71, 122
of Athena, Th 318, 896
of the gods, Th 389, 960, 993; WD 16
assembly (*boule*) of gods, Th 802

craft (*techne*), Th 160, 496, 864, 929; Prometheus' deceitful craft, Th 540, 547, 555, 560

Crete, 1-4, 9; Th 971; Th n102; birthplace of Zeus, 14, 18; Th 477, 480, 971

Cronus (Titan, father of Zeus, *see also* crooked-counseling) 10-14, 15, 109, 106, 107-9; Th 18; Th n57
child of Earth and Sky, hidden by Sky, Th 133-38, 154-9
castrates Sky at bidding of Earth, 110-11; Th 159-82; Th n64
imprisons Cyclopes and Hundred-Handed, 14; Th 502-7, 617-20
swallows children, 14, 18-19, 108-9; Th 453-67; Th n56, n63, n64, n65

tricked by Rhea and Earth, Th 467-500

Zeus, son of Cronus, 8, 112, Th 4, 53, 412, 423, 450, 534, 572, 624, 660, 949; WD 18, 69, 71, 138, 158, 168, 239, 242, 247, 259, 276

children of Cronus, Th 453, 625, 630, 634, 648, 668; Th n57

Cronus and golden age, WD 109-20; WD n10, n19

crooked-minded (*ankulometis, see also* intelligence), Cronus, Th 18, 137, 168, 473, 495
Prometheus, Th 546; WD 48

custom (*ethea*), Th 66; WD 136, 167, 222, 699; WD n14

Cyclopes (Circle-eyed, *see* Thunderer, Lightning and Brightness)
offspring of Earth and Sky, 3, 12, 14, 18; Th 139-46; Th n24, n66, n79

Cyprus, 4; Th 193, 199; Th n28

Cymatolege (a Nereid), Th 254

Cymo (a Nereid), Th 255

Cymodoce (a Nereid), Th 252

Cymopoleia (daughter of Poseidon), Th 819

Cymothoe (a Nereid), Th 245

Cyprogenes (Cyprus-born), Th 199; Th n28

Cythera, Th 192, 198; Th n28

Cytherea (epithet of Aphrodite), Th 196, 198, 934, 1008; Th n28

daimon, see spirit

Dark Age (the period 1200-800 in ancient Greece), 4, 9

dawn (*eos*), Th 451; WD 546-8, 578-80, 610, 724, 821; WD n65
daughter of Theia and Hyperion, Th 19, 372, 378, 381, 984; Th n90, n107

Dawn-bringer (*Eosphorus*) the Morning Star, daughter of Dawn and Astraeus (*see also* Stars) Th 381; Th n53

day (*hemera*), WD 102, 769, 822, 825
daughter of Erebus and Night, 12, 71, Th 124; with Night in Hades, Th 748-56
(*emar*), Th 59; WD 43, 176, 385, 488, 504, 524, 565, 597, 663, 667